Jennie McCarter

2

The Silver Dagger

by Allan Dwight

Spaniards' Mark
Drums in the Forest
The Silver Dagger

The
Silver
Dagger

by Allan Dwight

The Macmillan Company
New York   1959

Library of Congress catalog card number: 59-10988

The Macmillan Company, New York
Brett-Macmillan Ltd., Galt, Ontario

First Printing

PRINTED IN THE UNITED STATES OF AMERICA

To
Virginia Thompson Adloff
a small token

Contents

Contents

The
Mysterious
Mr. Galvez

MARK Woodbridge stood at attention on the pitching rolling deck and wished he were home in Connecticut. The rows of soldiers were jammed so tightly together not one could raise an arm. As the ship pitched steeply it was only the press of bodies that kept the lines upright, and as she rolled they swayed together. The rain was coming down in solid sheets of water. Lightning cracked up and down the masts, blinding the eyes with its vicious whiteness, and between the crashes of thunder the groaning of the timbers could be heard above the lash of waves. The fierce torrent of the wind bent the bare masts and ever hurled the ship forward into the unknown blackness.

For a moment the wall of rain lifted, and between the heads in front of him Mark could see a speck of tossing light. Then the rain fell again.

"Someone else's bad off as us," muttered a voice.

"No comfort in that," said another.

"I could have got this wet in Sharon," came from the back row.

"QUIET IN THE RANKS," bellowed a voice from

the poop, as a roll of thunder banged itself off to the west. "Two hours to dawn. Then we'll know where we are."

Two hours more of this! Mark shivered in his soaked uniform. At one time this joining the army had seemed the only way to get to Cuba and hunt for the Peneranda treasure. Now it seemed a harebrained and dangerous scheme. Why had he ever left the comfort and safety of Litchfield?

It had all begun that wet spring evening when the Spaniard who called himself Pedro Galvez came to the house.

Debby had just said goodnight to Elisha Tuttle, who was to marry her in June, and was setting the kitchen to rights, when there came a knock on the front door. "Elisha come back for something?" Mark asked.

Debby glanced around quickly. "Can't be. He didn't leave anything."

"Better light another lamp, then. I'll see who it is." Mark put his Virgil down on the settle.

Even though it was 1762, and Canada was now safely British, and even the Iroquois no longer raided down into Connecticut, one still opened the door cautiously to strangers. Particularly if it was a mile to the nearest farms and more than two to Litchfield.

Outside on the doorstep stood a figure in a black cape, a wide-brimmed black hat pulled down to the eyes. "Is this the house of John Woodbridge?" asked a smooth voice with an odd accent.

"It was," Mark answered shortly.

"Was? I am sorry. But may I come in? It is not Mr. Woodbridge but another I seek."

Grudgingly Mark opened the door and followed down the small boxed hall to the kitchen. Debby was standing, wide-eyed, the lamp still in her hands.

"My sister, Deborah, Mr . . . ?"

"Galvez, Pedro Galvez. Your servant, madam. I may take off my cape, no? Your rain in this country is gentle but very wet." He dropped the black cape across a ladder-back chair and placed his hat on top.

Debby's eyes were bright as she set the lamp on the table and dipped a little curtsey. The man was slender and clad in a black suit of a strange elegance, with silver buttons on the frogs of the coat and sleeves. He had smooth black hair and dark eyes half hidden by heavy white lids. As he pulled off his gloves Mark could tell that the white hands, with a heavy gold ring on one finger, had never done any farm work. Mark put his own large brown hands behind his back.

The man glanced from brother to sister questioningly. "My errand is brief. May I sit down? There are many hours of riding behind me." He crossed to the settle by the hearth. Mark sat down on the one opposite while Debby drew up a rocker and plumped Tabitha, the yellow cat, into her lap.

Mr. Galvez crossed one knee and placed the tips of his fingers together. "Your father?" he asked.

"Father died three months ago," Mark told him stiffly.

"Ah, so. My condolences. But, as I said, it is not him I seek." The words slid out softly, with that hint of an accent to give them importance. Mark felt a rising dislike for this figure and voice, but Debby was obviously impressed.

3

"I seek a relation."

"Don't have any." This man wouldn't learn anything, if Mark could help it.

"But I understood that your father had an uncle by the name of T'ad Benthon."

"Tad?" repeated Mark. "No one by that name."

"Oh, Mark, don't be stupid. He means Uncle Thaddeus Benson," cried Debby happily.

"Ah." Galvez looked at Debby. "That must be the man. Uncle?"

"He isn't Father's uncle, he's ours. Our mother's brother."

Mark wanted to kick Debby's shins to keep her quiet, but she was too far away.

"Yes. Of course. And I may see him?"

"No," said Mark before Debby could speak. Perhaps she'd take the hint and keep quiet. "You can't see him."

"No?" The arched eyebrows went up imperiously. "I understand not."

"Mark just means he isn't here," Debby put in swiftly. "He used to live with us, off and on, but the elders of the church objected to the way he used to drink and sing songs. They lectured at him and prayed over him until he said he couldn't stand it and went away."

"But where can I find him now?"

"Don't know." Mark had to drag out the words. He did not like this dark man. He turned and looked at Debby warningly, but she was smiling in a superior, sisterly fashion.

"Well, I know. He went to live at the poor farm two years ago. Said he could do what he wanted there, and take trips when he wished, and no one to bother him."

"The poor farm!" That was obviously unexpected. "You

4

mean a place for people who are . . . without means? But why should he . . . ? No matter. Miss Deborah, tell me where this poor farm can be found."

"It's over Torrington way, sir, some eight miles, on the road north from town. It's the Todman place, a house Mr. Todman left so old men would have a place to live out their days. Anyone can tell you. Uncle may be off on a trip, but likely not because the ground's too wet for traveling."

"I thank you. I have come a long way to talk with Mr. Benson." Mark held the black cape politely, though he would have preferred to let the man get into it himself. As Galvez held out his hand for his hat the lamplight fell on the gold ring. It held a green stone carved in a design that looked like a long knife with a ribbon circling the blade and hilt.

Galvez made another bow to Debby. "My gratitude to you for your information and my regrets for disturbing you." Instead of shaking hands with Debby properly, he bent over in a bow. Debby, delighted, curtseyed again.

Mark picked up a lamp and led the way to the front door. Galvez gave him a long look, nodded, and moved to the horse tied to the hitching post. Through the misting rain Mark watched him turn towards town.

"Why'd you tell that man where Uncle Thad was?" Mark burst out, back in the kitchen. "Couldn't you understand I wasn't going to let him find out anything?"

"But why not?" Debby smiled at him in an elder-sister way. "He had such nice manners I didn't see how you could be so rude and stupid. You showed you didn't like him, so I had to be extra polite. Though I don't understand why a man like that would come a long way to see Uncle Thad."

"I don't like it. He looked like a black snake to me."

5

"Perhaps he's someone Uncle Thad knew when he was off on those voyages," Debby went on, as if she hadn't heard. "Mother always said she couldn't understand him, coming back in rags and talking about adventures and his treasure."

"I told Mother she shouldn't let him go off to that poor farm." Mark paced the shadowy kitchen. "I wish he were here."

"He always liked you most of all."

"We got along best. I liked him, liked to do things with him, listen to his tales. They were wonderful, I remember, but I've sort of forgotten them now. And he'd seen more and done more than people here and looked at things differently."

"Made them wish they'd run off to sea and stayed away twenty years," giggled Debby. "But if he had any treasure it didn't do him any good."

"I'm going to see Uncle Thad tomorrow," Mark announced as he banked the fire. "I should have gone long ago. You remember he wasn't at that place when Elisha went to tell him about Father. Perhaps he doesn't know yet. I want to tell him about this man and ask him to come back and live here with us."

For just a second Debby looked dismayed. Then she smiled. "You go and ask him, Mark. Half the house is yours. And he'll be company for me while Elisha's working and you're at college, if you get to go, though I'm sure I don't know where the fees will come from. I'll really be glad to see Uncle Thad. Tell him I say to come."

By leaving just after daybreak Mark reached the poor farm at midmorning. It was a bleak, gray, square building with stark woods on two sides and at back. It looked both forlorn and forbidding. Mark shivered. What a place to end your days, even if you came of your own free will!

He followed the muddy path from the road around to the back door. Back of the house stood a sagging barn, with a group of men at one corner. Mark approached slowly. A squat, burly man stepped towards him.

"I've come to see Thaddeus Benson," said Mark. "Is he here?"

The man looked him over, then spoke around a spruce twig that drooped in the corner of his mouth. "Why? Who're you?"

"Mark Woodbridge, his nephew, from Litchfield."

The group of men was very still. Then a thin, white-haired man spoke up. "Thet's right, Jed. Thad used to talk about him. He's got the same gray eyes, black brows, brown hair, and wide face Thad had. Better let him see."

"See what?" Mark ran his tongue over his cold lips. "It's Uncle Thad I want."

"Yeup. Well, you're too late, sonny. Thad got hisself killed not over a half hour ago."

The men parted. Stiffly Mark moved towards a figure that was lying on the trodden snow. It was Uncle Thad. He was twisted as he lay, his hands clenched. Mark dropped on his knees and touched one of the brown hands. "What's happened?" he mumbled.

"We don't rightly know, sonny," answered the white-haired man. "After breakfast Thad went out to chop wood back of the barn."

"Thet's right," said a cracked voice. "I heerd him choppin' nice an' regular. It were his turn."

"I heerd him too," another man broke in. "I were in the

7

barn mendin' harness. First I heerd the choppin'. Then I heerd it stop. Thad was talkin' to someone. Didn't pay it no mind. Then I heerd Thad give a shout, then a sort of grunt. I run out, though I don't run so good with the wooden leg. When I git behind the barn there's Thad lyin' on the ground. Didn't think to look around I was thet surprised. I give a yell myself, an' went to fetch Jed."

"We started to take him to the house, but seed it weren't no use," continued Jed.

"But didn't anyone see anything?" asked Mark desperately.

"Nope. But Simon, he's lookin' around."

"But what killed him?"

"That there knife stickin' in his chest."

Mark made his head turn until he could see the worn coat. Something shone palely. It was a silver hilt of a dagger. He looked up at the impassive circle of faces. "But where'd that come from?"

"Ain't never seed it afore. Not Yankee work, neither."

"You got a plot to bury him in, sonny? We'll knock up a box fer him an' fetch him over, if you'll pay the county rate fer use of the horse." Jed's voice was kind but firm.

Mark could only nod. His throat was too tight for speech.

"Then there's no sense the two of you staying in the snow. We'll take him to the woodshed. You better git along back an' tell the preacher an' git the grave ready."

There was a stir among the men. Mark forced himself to look at Uncle Thad, who wasn't really Uncle Thad any more. He put his hand gently on the right hand and noticed vaguely that the skin of the knuckles was broken. The hand turned under his and something slid to the snow. Mark picked it up and put it in his pocket. It felt like a button. He stood up and looked around the circle. "Thank you all," he said hoarsely, and walked towards the bleak house and the lonely road home.

That night Mark and Debby sat again in front of the kitchen fire. Uncle Thad had been buried in the Woodbridge plot with the men from the poor farm and a few cronies from the tavern as the only other mourners. Throughout the short service "Why?" "Why?" had been ringing in the back of Mark's head. The words were still there, but he still had no answer. Outside the wind-blown rain pelted against the house.

"This won't make a difference in my marrying Elisha next June, will it, Mark?" Debby asked at last, timidly. "He said I was to ask you."

"Don't see why it should," Mark answered morosely. "We always said June was long enough to wait after Father died. No sense you and me living here alone."

"I'm glad you feel that way. I said you would."

Another gust shook the house, and as it died away there was knocking at the back door.

"Don't go," begged Debby nervously. "It might be that man again."

"Can't not go," Mark answered reasonably, but his feet dragged as he crossed the floor.

"Mark Woodbridge?" asked a dim figure. Mark nodded. That voice, at least, was New England. "I'd like to talk with you."

When the man had hung his heavy coat and fur cap on a peg he walked slowly across to Debby. "Name's Simon Etty, miss. Friend of your Uncle Thad. My sympathies."

He bent in what was not quite a bow, straightened, and looked at Mark. "And to you."

Mark held out his hand, and received a cautious shake. "Won't you sit down?" Debby asked tremulously. "Wouldn't you like a hot drink? We have a little tea."

"Wouldn't mind a drink, thank'ee. Don't need bought tea. No rum? Thought likely not. Sassafras tea's good. Clears the blood."

As Debby hurried to the cupboard Etty sat down on one of the settles. He was not much taller than Mark, and much thinner. His hair was grizzled and beneath thick gray eyebrows the two round blue eyes looked guileless. His skin was weatherbeaten, and his upper lip was long above a wide, slightly crooked mouth. He waited silently for Debby to bring the pewter mugs of hot tea, tasted his, nodded and thanked Debby.

"You didn't see me this morning," he began abruptly, looking across at Mark, " 'cause I wasn't there when you were. I was the one out tracking. When I got back you were gone. You're younger than I figgered, but can't be helped. Time'll take care of that. Come over in the cart and didn't go back. Wanted to see you."

"We're so glad to see a friend of Uncle Thad's," put in Debby. "You'll stay the night?"

Etty gave her a sudden pleased smile. "Glad to, miss. Got a lot to say." He drank half the tea and gave a quick shiver.

"I been figgering on what's my duty. Knew you're only relatives Thad had. Probably nothing can be done, but something ought to be." He looked back at Mark. "The way Thad got killed's mighty queer."

"I've been trying to figure out *why* ever since," Mark burst out.

"And the *how*'s as queer as the *why*. Now, you listen. There was no one around these parts who'd want to kill Thad. He kept his distance, but he was well liked. He told tall tales, but the men liked that, too, though they didn't believe much. No reason to kill there. And he didn't have anything anyone would want to kill him for, living at the Todman place winters, working odd jobs, hunting, trapping around rest of the time. So, I can't answer the *why* now."

Mark nodded agreement. It was a relief to have someone talk about the mystery so simply and clearly.

"But there's the *how*. Thad was talking to someone back of the barn. When I saw he was dead I went to look. A man wearing an uncommon narrow boot had come walking out of the woods, come across to Thad. They'd stood a piece. Then they'd set down on the woodpile. Then they'd jumped up. Thad had started to back away towards the corner of the barn. The man must have hit him, 'cause Thad's cheek was bruised. Thad must have yelled then and hit back. And that's when the man must have stuck the fancy knife in him. Thad grabbed at him, but couldn't hold on. The man ran back to the woods, around a thicket to where he had a horse tied to an oak sapling. Horse headed back through the woods, south, the way he had come, and got back on the road after a half mile. All that was written in the snow, from that little fall after the rain.

"So, figgering the boots, *and* the horse, *and* the fancy knife, it adds up to someone who doesn't belong in these parts. But Thad talked with him, so Thad must have known him, or the man said something so Thad wasn't suspicious. So it figgers out to someone Thad met in furrin parts. Did he ever talk about anyone who might want to kill him?"

Mark shook his head. "It was two years ago he was here

the last time, Mr. Etty. He used to talk about his adventures in the West Indies some, but not much about people, unless he was minded of a funny story. I—I used to like to hear him."

"Can't abide having Thad's kin call me Mr. Etty. Plain Simon it is to my friends, which you are because of Thad. He spoke well of you, Mark, and of your sister too. I figgered he wasn't likely to tell you much until you were more grown, but no harm asking, as the drunk said to the scarecrow. But if anyone's going to do anything about it, any time, it'll have to be you and me, son. So I bring you this funny knife. It might help you find that man."

From the side pocket of his jacket he pulled the silver dagger. Mark turned his eyes away. He could see Uncle Thad this minute, with the silver hilt shining in the pale sunlight.

"Don't do that, son." Simon's voice was gentle. "If you start by not looking at something you don't like it'll get harder to look each time. Tell yourself there's no reason why you can't look. It's just a fancy knife you're going to keep by you. Take it."

Mark put out his hand hesitantly, then quickly seized the hilt. The steel blade gleamed evilly. There was a carving on the smooth hilt but he did not look at it.

"Now," shot out Simon, "let me see what it was you picked up from Thad's hand and put in your pocket. Jed said he saw you do it, but didn't like to say anything."

Mark stared, perplexed, then he remembered, and from the side pocket of his coat brought out a round button. In the light it shone silver. Simon looked at it with satisfaction.

"Knew Thad had grabbed him as he fell. Purty thing. Never seen a button like it."

Mark held it to the lamp. Engraved on the rounded top was a design of a dagger with a ribbon flowing around and over it. He turned to the dagger. On the hilt was engraved the same design. On the ribbon he could distinguish the words "Semper vinco." Dimly he heard Simon say, "I've voyaged some myself. Know a bit of Spanish. That dagger was made in Spain."

Mark stared at the design. "The words are Latin," he said slowly. "They mean 'I always conquer.'" He could not take his eyes from the design. The same dagger and ribbon had been carved on the green stone in the ring on the hand of the mysterious Mr. Galvez.

2

Uncle Thad's Story

THE big four-poster bed in the front room was wide enough for three people. Though Mark would not have admitted it, he was glad to have Simon for company that night. Debby had gone cheerfully to her room across the narrow hall, but then Debby hadn't seen Uncle Thad lying on the snow. Mark thought he wouldn't sleep easily, but he was off even before Simon had climbed in beside him.

Something poked him awake. A voice in the blackness was whispering in his ear. "Don't move. Don't make a noise. Someone's downstairs. Your sister?"

Mark shook his head, then murmured "No." He could feel Simon sit up. From below came a muffled stirring, so faint he would never have heard it in his sleep.

"I'm going down," whispered Simon. "If you can't move like a mink you better stay here."

The bed raised as a weight was removed. Mark knew he couldn't move like a mink, but he couldn't let this man go alone downstairs. As he stood on the rag rug a faint movement of air told him the bedroom door was open. As he crossed the floor a board sighed; he hoped the wind and rain on the windows covered the noise.

The hall was as black as the bedroom. How had Simon gone down the steep stairs without a creak? A cold drift of air told Mark the front door was ajar. Step by step he went down, leaning against the wall to ease his weight. A soft thud came from the parlor.

"We'll rush him together," came in a whisper so soft he could hardly hear it. Behind Simon he moved towards the room.

"Come on, Mark, Sam, Ben," shouted Simon. "Get him."

There was a crash, a thud of bodies colliding, a sudden grunt, and an unseen shoulder struck him so heavily he was knocked asprawl. Wind rushed through the house as the door opened and was slammed. As Mark got to the door he heard hoofbeats, galloping.

Debby was coming down the stairs, candle in hand. "Mark! What's the matter?"

"Light a lamp in the parlor, quick."

The candle showed one of the windsor chairs lying on its side, half in, half out of the doorway, and Simon sitting on the floor. The lamp showed that every drawer of the Governor Winthrop desk and the highboy had been turned upside down, the contents spread over the room. The two portraits had been jerked from the wall, the rag rugs turned over. Simon was holding his shoulder, blood oozing between his fingers.

"Right smart man," said Simon thoughtfully. "Smart enough to put that chair in the doorway for me to stumble over. I should have been looking for such tricks, but I wasn't."

"Come in the kitchen and I'll bathe that cut," Debby told

him composedly. "I'll straighten this in the morning. Mark, stir up the fire."

The cut was just at the top of his shoulder where it did little harm. Debby bathed and bandaged it deftly and then made some more sassafras tea.

"What was he after, Mark?" Simon asked over his mug.

"Don't know." Mark's dark eyebrows drew together. "Everyone around here knows we don't have any money. You couldn't see him?"

"Nope. Too black. I fell nicely over that chair, which gave him the warning he wanted. He came right at me. Never thought of a knife or I might have stopped it. Likely he could see enough, been in the dark so long, for he aimed where the heart would have been if I hadn't slipped to one side. Your coming, Mark, made him beat it."

Mark rubbed his shoulder. "Could you feel anything?"

"Felt the knife some." Simon's long face quirked into a smile. "Felt a cloak, or something loose hanging on him, when I grabbed for his arm. Good cloth."

"That sounds like Galvez," said Mark slowly. And, with interruptions from Debby, he told about the visit the night before.

"Yup. No proof, though, but it stands to reason." He cocked his head on one side. "Come after Thad. Got Thad. Come back for something. But what?"

Debby, her face still pale under her mob cap, suddenly clapped her hands over her mouth. "I know," she cried. "The chest. Uncle Thad left his sea chest with Mother."

Simon nodded. "As good a guess as any." He set his mug on the table. "Tell you what. Tomorrow I'll mosey into town. See if I can find anything about a stranger. If I can't, I'll go on to New Haven. That's where a body would start from, if looking for someone in these parts. I'll be back soon as I can. You, Mark, you go through that chest. Know where it is?"

Both Debby and Mark shook their heads.

"You'll find it. Connecticuters don't throw anything away. See what's in there a furriner might want."

The wind and the rain had cleared into a soft sunny day that said spring had practically arrived. Looking through the window to the sky Mark could tell that the willows by the brook would turn pale green in a day or so and it was already time to start plowing. He turned to Simon, but the bed was empty.

"He was gone before I was up," Debby told him over the corn meal mush. "I never heard him leave, either." Although she looked tired, her blue eyes were bright and her brown curls were fluffed around her face. Mark thought, again, that Elisha would be getting a pretty wife as well as a good one. He started to tell her so and stopped. It was hard to say such things to anyone, even a sister.

"When you've taken care of Hebe and brought in the wood why don't you go look for the chest?" she suggested. "It's my guess it's in the attic."

When Hebe was milked and taken to the common pasture and the woodbox filled, Mark started for the attic. It was as wide and as long as the two front rooms of the house with a back roof that sloped steeply down to the kitchen. Two small windows at each end lighted the place that smelled of old leather, dried apples, herbs, and dry timber.

Mark had always avoided the attic since his mother's death, for so many times he had helped her turn the slices of apples, or hang the clusters of herbs, or fetched the extra quilts, that it seemed too much a part of his life with her for him to face. But even though he could almost see her slender figure in the blue checked dress and white apron he was not so oppressed as before by his loss. Now he had to find Uncle Thad's sea chest.

He found his great grandmother's big spinning wheel, too old-fashioned now for Debby, a broken corn husker he had always said he would mend and had forgotten, a baby's sleigh on runners, a four-poster for which there was no room, and the pine chest that held the quilts and linen. Uncle Thad's chest had been small and dark. At last he came on it, under the farthest eaves and back of a string bed too small for Debby.

As he carried it on his shoulder down to his room Uncle Thad's voice was with him. "I'm leaving my sea chest here, lad," he had said that May morning two years ago. "I'll be back for it, never fear. But if I don't make this port again everything in it's yours, and maybe there's something in it you'll find mighty interesting someday. But I'll be telling you about it all when you're a bit older and got more meat on your bones."

They had been standing under the elms by the gate. "Why do you go?" Mark had managed to ask. He knew it was unmanly to cry, but he couldn't keep the tears out of his eyes.

He could almost feel now the comforting weight of his uncle's arm on his shoulder. "In part it's my itching foot, Mark, and in part it's my pride. I've never been a burden to anyone, and I won't be now. And it would worry your mother, me here a bit and off to hunt and back again, and off, and the church people clacking and yawping at her about me. Your father understands, though he doesn't feel the same way. Sometimes I've thought it's a pity he took to teaching, he'd have made a good fighter, or a good law-yer. You're growing into quite a lad yourself, and in a few years we'll set things right, the two of us, and get what's rightfully ours. And we'll be the biggest cocks in the state, if money can make us so."

Mark was surprised to find he remembered every word. Perhaps all the memorizing his father had made him do had been a help.

Uncle Thad had come back just once, with a peddler's pack, saying that if he couldn't sail the seas he could walk the roads and see new places that way. He had had a bite and patted Mark. "You're growing fast, Tadpole. We'll be off in a year or so." He had winked and turned down the road and there had been no chance to ask him more. And that was the last time Mark had seen him until he lay with the Spanish dagger in his heart.

Mark lowered the chest to the floor by the window and sat down beside it. The rope that bound it was stiff with age and tar and he had to cut it to pull up the lid. What he had expected he could not have said, but not a pair of worn trousers of tanned cowhide and a knit stocking cap. Underneath was a white waistcoat embroidered with red roses and a black broadcloth suit with silver buttons that looked almost new. Then came a box that held a pair of pistols with ivory handles and neat compartments for bul-lets and powder, tinder and flint and ramrod. Somehow the pistols did not go with the stocky, homey figure of Uncle Thad.

At the bottom was a bundle wrapped in a dark cloth, an oblong box dark with tarnish. Inside was first a sheet of

19

fresh white paper which, when unfolded, was a simple will. "To my nephew, Mark Woodbridge, I leave all of which I die possessed or anything of any nature whatsoever which may come to me in any manner after my death." This was duly witnessed by the Reverend Morton and John Avery, and dated two years ago.

Beneath, wrapped in white silk, were two sets of papers. One was a large document on heavy parchment with a red seal at the bottom, written in very black ink and in a language that was neither English nor Latin. He could make nothing of it except the name Thaddeus Benson and Connecticut repeated several times. He laid it aside and picked up the other paper. When he saw *Dear Nephew Mark* he settled his shoulder against the window and began to read.

These six months I have spent with your mother and father have been made particularly pleasant, my dear boy, by your comradeship. During our hours together I have observed you closely. Though you are but a lad I have felt that I have discerned promise of your developing steadfastness, intelligence and courage that augur well for your future and for the enterprise I have in mind for us to undertake together. Though you have listened most properly to my tales, I realize you are over young to be burdened with these plans for claiming my, and your, inheritance. I hope to tell you of them in a few years. But, as the Reverend Mr. Morton put it so forcibly in his somewhat over-long sermon on Sunday, man is but mortal, he flourisheth like a flower and like a flower is cut down. On pondering his words, during the remainder of his discourse, I felt the weight of my years, and my duty was shown clearly to me. Therefore, I leave this account for you, along with the deed of Don Diego, so that if aught should befall me you will know, if not all, enough, so that, with the counsel of your wise and esteemed parents, you may lay out your course of action. This, then, is the story.

Mark dropped the paper to his lap and looked around the familiar room. This was the Uncle Thad who had spent two years at Harvard, not the easy-going Uncle Thad he had known. He wished he had had time to know both Uncle Thads. The elegant handwriting, with its flourishes, was hard to read. Uncle Thad had been sent down from Harvard for winning his bet that he could walk the ridge-pole of Massachusetts Hall, had run away to sea rather than face the wrath of his father, and not been heard of for ten years. Then he had only come back for an occasional brief visit until the leg that had not been set properly had, he said, land-bound him for good. Mark felt a lump in his throat, and bent his brown head over the crowded pages.

There is no point in setting down even a portion of my experiences at sea. They tell better than they write. For thirty years I sailed with the privateers who haunted the blue waters, white cities and green isles of the Caribbean. I have seen more than my share of blood and death, of bravery and cowardice, cupidity and generosity. Once, indeed, I had my own ship, with flags of five nations I could change at will, and would have had it still had not pride and vanity, those temptations I could not always resist, told me I could outshoot and outsail the Spaniard, Black Rodrigo.

Yet, in a way, it was both pride and vanity that brought to me the fortune and future you and I will share.

It was when I was first mate aboard the brigantine,

Gloria, *whose memory is best forgotten. Politeness would name her a privateer, but truth would name her pirate. Any ship of any size was our prey, for these were no longer the days of the great Morgan when only a Spanish plate ship was a worthy victim. One afternoon off the eastern point of Cuba we found a heavy, square-sterned Spanish brig lumbering westward. A lucky shot brought down her main-mast and we boarded her. There was fighting aplenty to keep our crew of ruffians occupied. Chance, or fate, led me to the dim cabin beneath the poop. And there an old voice said in Spanish, 'If Antonio had not taken my pistols I would shoot you. If you are a man, try to kill me with your sword.'*

Sitting up in bed was an old man with white hair and a small, pointed white beard. In his right hand he held a long rapier. 'I'm a better man with one leg than you with two,' he went on softly. 'Try, my bravo, and see.' He raised his rapier. Light from the little window ran along the bright blade to the needle-sharp point, and his eyes were just as bright. From overhead, muffled, could be heard shouts and screams and trampling of men.

I did have a pistol and I could have shot him. But there was something about him, alone and in bed and not afraid, that I liked. Also, he looked a little like my father, who had been a man, too, but of different temper.

Suddenly I laughed. 'I will not shoot you,' I said, 'nor will I let you kill me with that long sword, as well you might.' (I could see that pleased him.) 'Furthermore, I will not let anyone else shoot you. Is your leg gone?'

He courteously lowered the tip of the rapier. 'No. It was broken on the stairs in a gale last week. If you will neither kill me nor fight me I must be your prisoner. But, I warn you, there is little gold in this cabin.'

'Never mind,' I told him impudently. 'I'd rather have you as my share of the loot than any wench or jewel.'

So the old gentleman became, indeed, my share, and I insisted on carrying him to our ship where I cared for him. Later, when we picked up a coasting sloop, I put him and myself in it and set sail for Cuba. The winds were not trustworthy, and we were long in reaching Havana. Why I acted thus, to this day I know not. Mayhap I was weary of pirating, of money that went more quickly than it was gained. Mayhap I was weary of my comrades, for they were never comrades in the true sense. This gentleman, wise as the old who had seen and remembered much are wise, was educated far beyond any dreams of those self-important professors at Harvard. So much had he read and seen that I did delight to listen to his tales by the hour, for it was of many new worlds he spoke to me.

His name was Diego Ippolito Alexandre Rodriguez Pene-randa y Salvatierra. His wife and children were dead; he spoke of them but little. His favorite estate lay to the east of the city of Havana. It was there we steered, and from a little shallow bay, with the aid of some chance-met peons, I carried him to his home.

For four years I lived with him, at times at the massive Casa Peneranda in Havana, in summers at Casa Alta in the hills, or we journeyed to his other estates. But of them all he preferred the Casa Hermosa, east of Havana by the sea. And out of courtesy to me he had all his house servants and slaves taught English so I could talk with them more easily, for the Spanish language was difficult for me.

In all things he treated me as the son he had lost, and in full measure I returned his affection. He was a great gentleman. Then, when he knew he was dying, he sent for his lawyer and also the Mayor of Havana, and made a new will. One copy I leave with this letter. One remained in Diego's strong box. The other went with the Mayor. He left to me the Casa Hermosa, its land, and anything in the ground that I might find. The many other estancias around the island and the Havana house went to two nephews.

Don Diego had had one brother who had left two sons who expected to inherit all. In the beginning, when Don Diego returned with me, the two dark and evil young men came posthaste from Havana. They ordered me from the place, but Diego left them no doubts that he was still the master, and it was they who left. But they hated me henceforth, and twice tried to kill me. Thrice they came by night to search for the jewels, but our watch was good, though they escaped.

For there were many jewels that formed the Peneranda Hoard. Some had come from Don Diego's wife, a Spanish lady of great fortune. Many more had come through the family of Peneranda, from Spain and from the New World. There were rings torn from Aztec fingers and crowns snatched from Inca heads. For ease of keeping, most of the jewels were unset. We treasured them for their color and beauty more than for their worth. As his last illness approached Don Diego became fearful for me when alone in a strange land and surrounded by powerful enemies. He was determined, as only a Spaniard, the most stubborn of people, can be determined, that the jewels would be mine. So one night we buried the Hoard in our own chest. The place I hope to show you, but, if that should not come to pass one direction I can leave you. In the Salle Grande at Casa Hermosa hangs a portrait of Don Diego when a young man. It is a fine portrait that I hope we can someday hang in our own home. Moreover, it has a strange and unique frame. Should it be necessary, examine this frame most closely, for future guidance. What you will find will tell you what you need to know. With the Hoard will be found my own few jewels, for I could do no less than lay mine with Diego's.

So, Don Diego died and was buried, and I was accepted as master by his people. With the aid of Beltran, his confidant and foreman, I conducted the affairs of the estate, in which I had helped for four years. This Beltran I must mention. Part Indian, probably Mayan, and part Spanish, he was our friend and he will be yours. He had travelled with Don Diego and already spoke English well and some French. Strong and fearless, honest but cunning, he is a man who could have made his own mark if his lot had been cast in other times and places. It was he who persuaded Diego that it would be a matter of courtesy to teach the Peneranda people English, since my Spanish was not too fluent. Twice Beltran saved my life, and once I saved his. I would have done more for him, but I did persuade Diego to free him and give him his own land. The Spaniards, I have long observed, are cruel, but much of their cruelty comes from lack of thought and imagination. In this way, by pointing out to Diego, who was a kindly intentioned man, something he had not thought to notice, I could soften in part the life of his people, and many of them he freed gladly when persuaded of their virtue.

It was the gratitude of these freed slaves that a last time saved my life. At the reading of the will of Don Diego the nephews, though he had left each a share of the remaining jewels and gold plate as well as the estates, swore I would not long enjoy my inheritance. The lawyer bravely pointed out that one copy of the will was mine, one now with him, and one with the Mayor, and the nephews could do nothing. But three months later they came with bravos to help them. Unknown to me, Beltran had always kept watch, fearing this thing.

Beltran roused me, and though my inclination was to stay and fight for my people and my rights, he persuaded me that this was not wise. I must flee, and he would send me word when I could safely and peacefully return. So, while others fought for me, Beltran lead me to the shore and his own dory. As you can well imagine, Mark, there was no time to seek out the hidden Hoard. The men attacking the Casa were inflamed with liquor and I feared for the safety of the people and of the house Don Diego had loved so well. So, to my sometimes regret, I fled, with little but enough to buy my passage north. That night I rowed eastward (Havana would have been certain death) and a day later was picked up by a barkentine out of Newport on her last leg home.

Since then I have waited for word that I should return. Beltran, an honorable man, would tell me, and would write in care of your father. When it is proper he will. Now those peaceful sunlit years in Cuba seem more like a dream than a reality. But now I dream that we will go together and live happily at the Casa Hermosa. If God wills otherwise, I have left this for your guidance and my copy of

Don Diego's will. But I count the months until I may show you my inheritance, which shall be yours.

Your aff't Uncle
Thaddeus Benson

Post scriptum. If you should indeed be compelled to return alone, give to Beltran a double handful of the jewels. He helped me bury them. He will use his share wisely.

It was past noon when Mark finished the crowded pages. Carefully he hid letter and will in the chest and returned it to the darkest corner of the attic. But now what should he do? He could not doubt Uncle Thad's story for a moment, and there was the will he could not read as proof. He could not talk to Debby. She would laugh at it all as moonshine and counsel him to forget it.

But somehow he must get to Cuba. There were not two pounds in the house, and he could see no way to earn enough for his passage. As he began to plow the cornfield he suddenly remembered Simon Etty. The picture of the thin man with the bright blue eyes suddenly brought comfort. Surely he would have some sound advice and dry wisdom.

3

One Way
to Cuba

SIMON Etty was back the next afternoon for supper. Over the stew and johnny cake he told Mark and Debby that he had been as far as New Haven, by hooking rides here and there, and had come on the trail of the man who called himself Galvez. He had come by stage from New York, hired a horse and returned two days later, and then taken the stage back to New York. He had spoken little, even in the tavern.

Mark had already made up his mind not to say anything to Debby about what he had found in Uncle Thad's sea chest until he had had a chance to talk to Simon. And Debby seemed to have forgotten it all, for Elisha Tuttle was coming to call this evening and she was in a bustle to set things to rights. Once Simon had disposed of Galvez he began to talk about the weather, all sorts of weather, even going back to snow storms and spring floods in his childhood in Massachusetts. It was evident he had something else to discuss, but not in front of Debby. Her cheeks pink and her eyes laughing, she fairly brushed them out of the kitchen with the birch broom.

It was a warm evening, with the western sky turning lemon yellow and the breeze bringing a fresh, dank smell from the woods. Simon nodded toward the stone wall beside the barn. "We can talk there," he suggested, "and no one can hear."

Once settled, he filled his pipe painstakingly, looking over it at Mark. "You'll do all right," nodded Simon. "You got good eyes and nose and chin, just like Thad had, and you're a might broader already."

Mark felt himself blushing. "I'd like to be like my father and Uncle Thad."

"You'll be better than either of them, not that they weren't fine men, you understand. But you'll know more and different things, and mind you use what you know. And that's what we got to do now.

"I been turning over in my mind what to do about Thad. It's against human instinct to have your kin or your friend knifed to death and not do something about it. As I kept churning away inside my head I began to remember some of the tales Thad told, when he was in the mood to talk. Some I don't believe to this day, but some, I bet, were the unvarnished truth. It's the most unlikely ones that are apt to be the truth.

"Now I fished among them unlikely tales for some reason for a man from furrin parts to kill Thad. He'd knifed a drunken sailor in some French port. Nothing there. He'd run guns into some little Spanish countries. But a mort of people have done that, and not got knifed. No. It had to be something personal. Then I hit on it.

"Must have been two years ago come next October. We were in the mountains north of Albany to see if we could pick up some beaver. It'd turned cold, and we'd found ourselves a right neat little hidey hole under a ledge, and fixed ourselves as nice a rabbit as you ever tasted. We'd come to talking about guns, and then other ways of killing, and come to knives, and it was the knife that brought it back to me.

"Thad said Spanish steel was the best in the world, and he'd gone on rambling until he came to his tale about Cuba. Then he really got started. Told me how he'd saved the life of some high old cockalorum down there, and been treated like a son afterwards. The old gent died, leaving a lot of his goods to Thad, but it hadn't done Thad much good, for he'd been run out by the kinfolk, though his having the place was all legal and proper. Now, there'd be people who didn't like Thad personal. You'll say there's no reason to come traipsing up here after all these years to kill poor Thad. And I'd say something might have happened, or they might have been afraid something was going to happen, to make them want to be sure Thad was a goner.

"So the more I pondered the more it seems like the place to go is Cuba . . ."

Mark had jumped from the wall, his boots squelching in the muddy grass. "You're right, sir," he interrupted. "And you've about figured it out, too. Let me tell you . . ."

Simon nodded and let out a puff of blue smoke. "Knew it as I watched your face. Shouldn't let your face give away so much what you're thinking and feeling, son. But you'll learn, as the schoolmaster said as he laid on the cane. So you found something in Thad's chest?"

Sitting again on the wall, Mark poured out all of Uncle Thad's letter, while Simon puffed and nodded. "Yup, that's it, son. Acorns to doubloons that Galvez is a Peneranda."

"And now I don't know what to do. I . . . I have to

take care of Debby. But I want to do something about Uncle Thad, and that place, and the Hoard. I feel so stupid."

"You aren't stupid, boy," Simon said comfortingly. "You've just never had a chance to find out how good you can be. You've been took care of, up to now, never had to think much or do much except what you're told. Never had to both think *and* act. There's a heap of men can act, strong men who can knock in a fellow's nose or heist a millstone. There's a heap as can think *and* talk your ear off. But a man needs to be able to think *and* act, but he won't know if he can as long as he's kept wrapped up in wool. A man's just got to find out for himself how good he is, but when he finds out he doesn't let anyone else know he knows."

Mark moved restlessly. The sky had paled to a clear light that was the absence of all color. Darkness was creeping in from the woods and gathering beneath bushes and trees. Overhead one star shone feebly. The stone beneath him was suddenly hard and cold. "You're right," he mumbled. "I know I've had it easy. I've got to go to Cuba. But there's Debby."

"Got an answer to that." He jerked his head toward the yellow light behind the small-paned window of the kitchen. "This young Tuttle now. Your father liked him?"

"Oh, yes. Elisha'd asked for Debby before father died. They're just waiting for the proper time to pass."

"See if they won't get hitched next month. That's long enough to wait, and he won't be so far behind on the spring planting. Then your mind's free about Debby. As for Cuba, now. That's easy, too. Found out in John Waite's tavern in New Haven. I'd stopped in to wet my whistle when in comes Ben Stockton that was with me under

31

Abercrombie. He's been with some officer on Amherst's staff. No one is supposed to know staff plans, but Ben's always had ears like an owl. We've licked the Frenchies and now we got to lick the Spaniards. England's sending an army and a fleet, and these colonies are going to be asked to send some regiments. And where do you think we're going to fight the Dons? Right at Havana, so as to take over Cuba. It took three beers to get it out of Ben, he's tight-lipped as a Mohawk, but it's straight. That's where any provincial regiments are going to be sent, come June or July."

"I know there's been a war in Europe and England's fighting France and Spain. But I don't see . . ."

Simon stood up and pointed his pipe. "Wake up, son. There's a free trip to Havana, all for taking the King's shilling. Enlist. See? Won't be much of a fight, probably. The Dons say they licked the world once, but I've never seen them licking much more'n an alley cat, myself. Then, when the fighting's over, we can find out about this Don Diego and your Uncle Thad's place. I've heard tell they talk a funny Spanish in Cuba, and mine's funny enough to make a cow laugh, so we ought to get along well enough to learn what we need to know."

"Where do we sail from?"

"The regiments? Ben says from New York."

Mark rose and stuck out his hand. "It's a bargain. And in New York there'll be someone who can read Spanish and tell us what the will really does say, so we'll know where we stand. We'll take the will with us and we can go to court there and everything will be simple."

"Well," Simon drawled as he shook hands. "It's a bargain on enlisting, and getting the will read in New York.

But if I were you I wouldn't count on them courts just handing things over to a furriner. Other countries don't look at the law same as we do. We may have to do some taking on our own, as the fox said when he nipped off with a goose."

On the eighteenth of May Simon returned. Debby had been married for two weeks, and Mark and Elisha together had the spring work well in hand. Both Debby and the farm would be safe with the quiet, steady Elisha. Debby had cried and said even though he was tall he didn't know enough about fighting to be a soldier and sixteen was too young, but of course he must do what he thought right. Mark's shoulder-pack was ready, but he had not yet decided the safest place to carry the will.

"You got any money?" asked Simon. "Fifteen shillings? Well, bring it. In New Haven we'll get one of those belts sailors wear. It opens up and will hold flat that piece of paper. You can put your money in it, too, if you like. If a thief hits you on the head he usually doesn't have time to do more than go through your pockets. Me, I keep my money in my sock. Makes for kind of hard walking, but at least I always know it's there."

Mark did get a belt in New Haven. He had copied the will as best he could and left the copy in the chest in the attic, along with the original of Uncle Thad's letter, and told Debby they were very important and he would write later, if he needed them. A copy of the important part of Uncle Thad's letter he kept with him.

Enlisting was simple and not at all as exciting as Mark had expected. On the twentieth they were approaching New London and the schooner *Speedwell* which would

33

take them to New York. Simon had learned that the Connecticut troops, if not all the Provincials, would be under Colonel Lyman of Northampton and Colonel Israel Putnam, and said both were good men. Both had done some fighting against the French and Indians, and that was a help.

"Don't ever stay under any officer that hasn't had experience," he warned. "It's better to desert and get shot, for that's quick, and you're likely to die anyway, but more unpleasant under a young squirt who doesn't know anything and thinks he knows everything." But Mark was looking eagerly down at the blue harbor and green shores and the haze beyond that was Long Island, and did not listen. He had never been so far from home before.

On the twenty-first they set sail down the Sound on a dull voyage westward. The schooner was crowded with men of all ages, all from Connecticut, and all tight-lipped. Judging by their expressions they were not interested in where they were going or why, and disapproved of everything about them, yet all were volunteers. Simon allowed it was just the Connecticut way of acting; they didn't like anything outside their own colony and not much in it, except their own town, and not all of that.

On the twenty-fourth they passed through Hellgate, the dangerous and famous narrows where Long Island came nearest to the New York shore. Here the currents were swift and confused, and a ledge of rock was visible in the channel even at high tide. Once through the narrows, guided by a special pilot who put on airs, they moved down the East River between the wooded hills of Manhattan and the farms to the east. On the west shore were large country houses with gardens, and once a glimpse of the

Boston road, but not until the tip of the island was nearly reached was the city of New York visible.

At first the country places were a little closer together; then came taverns or public gardens, and at last the solid ranks of city houses. They were high and straight and severe looking, with dormer windows set in steep roofs that rose stiffly above the two floors, and chimneys at each end. Many had a long series of steps on each gable, which, Simon said, weren't steps but just the Dutch idea of decoration. Along the shore were slips, filled with water running inland, or wharfs built out into the river. As the east wind pushed them slowly past the city, Mark counted five church spires and one rounded cupola that someone said was the dome of the city hall. At the end of the island was the fort, with brick barracks and a fine house for the governor inside its thick walls. Mark hoped they would tie up at the city, but they passed on out into a wide bay. The heights of Brooklyn fell away to their left and now he could see Hudson's river, and, upstream, the straight cliffs and wooded heights of New Jersey. The *Speedwell* passed a little flat island and at last dropped anchor at Staten Island.

4

Mark
Makes a
Mistake

FOR the next ten days Mark could do nothing but move as he was told and sleep exhaustedly at night.

The first day each man received his uniform and arms and an allotment of food. Mark thought the brown breeches, brown coat cut square at the knees, yellow waistcoat, white shirt and black tricorne were as fine a uniform as one could ask. But Tom Davidson, a cheerful, tall, gawky lad from Granby who slept and ate next to him, complained that the buff and blue of the New York Provincials, or the gaudy red breeches and blue coats of the Royal Americans would help them get all the girls. Each soldier was given a musket that came as high as Mark's shoulder, with powder horn and strap to sling over his left shoulder, and canteen.

Thereafter it was drill all day and sleep in brush shelters at night. Slowly the ragged lines of men began to march more evenly and the muskets to move with precision, though the drill sergeant, a down East man with a voice like a file, swore they were the laziest bunch of loggerheads Connecticut had ever gladly shipped out of the state. The only diversion was the flogging of fifteen deserters, done in a hollow square before the entire Provincial army. After that there was no more grumbling about the food or the steady drilling.

Mark was impatient to get into town. He had counted on going with Simon, but the day he was given a six hour pass Simon was assigned to the Colonel's guard.

"Sure you can make your way around alone?" Simon asked anxiously as he polished his boots. "A city can be a fearsome thing, the first time."

"There's nothing to it," Mark answered impatiently. "I'll just walk along until I find a sign about Spanish and get a translation written out. I want to know just what was left to Uncle Thad and if there are any conditions or . . . or anything."

Simon set his tricorne at a slight tilt that made his long face look rakish, and nodded. "Look out for yourself," he advised in a neutral voice, and was gone.

A flat scow took the men on leave across the tumbling waters to the dock near the square fort. One of the men said on the way over that more than seventeen thousand people lived in New York, but he was jeered into silence. Most of them were talking of sports and taverns and how far would a shilling carry them. Several asked Mark to join them, but he said he had business and would see them later.

It was a warm, bright afternoon, with the scent of the locust blossoms mingling with that of fish, salt water, tar from a rope walk, spices and manure. Mark had never seen so many houses or paved streets, and his inclination was to stroll and gawk at everything. Instead, he hurried across the open space one of the soldiers called the Bowling Green toward a narrow cobbled street that looked as though it should lead to the business section. Here, on the first floors of the narrow houses, he found the stores, each with its sign to show its goods. A small chair swinging from an arm above a door obviously was a cabinetmaker, a teapot betokened a goldsmith, a key an ironmonger, and a pair of breeches topped by a sun a tailor.

He had crossed one street and was hesitating where to turn when, looking up, he saw a small sign "Adam Shuttleworth, Counselor at Law." Abruptly he changed his search. It would be practically impossible, he now realized, for him to find anyone in the city who spoke Spanish, at least without help and in the six hours allowed. Perhaps what he really needed was a lawyer.

A slit of a door beside the window of an ironmonger opened to dark precipitate stairs. A tiny landing at the top held only one closed door. Within arguing voices stopped as he knocked.

"Come," was called impatiently, and he pushed open the door.

The room was small and low-ceilinged. The blue walls were as dirty as the two square windows. At a desk in front of the windows sat a man in a black suit. His round, full-cheeked face should have been ruddy but was curiously white, and held a pair of small brown eyes above a button nose and a pursed mouth.

He looked at Mark in surprise. "What brings you here?" he demanded harshly.

Mark felt himself grow red and nearly turned to leave. But how could he find another lawyer? Perhaps all lawyers were like this. "A will, sir," he stammered.

"A will?" The voice changed to a soft purr. "Well, well. What have you been left and who are you?"

"I'm Mark Woodbridge, of Connecticut, sir."

"Well, come sit down in that chair. And this is my-er-cousin, Robert Lamson."

Now Mark noticed a uniformed man with carroty hair, neatly clubbed, and pale blue eyes sitting slouched in a slat-backed chair in the corner.

"Let's see the will." Mr. Shuttleworth's little mouth was stretched in a smile, but his eyes were watchful. "You'll find no one in the colonies more experienced with wills, I assure you."

Mark unbuttoned his coat and pulled the packet from the place in his belt. "It's from my uncle, a will that was left to him. But it's in Spanish, sir." He smoothed the heavy parchment and laid it on the table.

Shuttleworth leaned forward quickly. "You were lucky, young man, to find me, for few in the city know that language. But Captain Lamson knows it. Robert, come see what you can make of this."

Languidly the man rose and came to the table. "Spanish it is," he said in a neutral voice. "See, Adam, Havana, 1758 it says. Here's his name . . . he's leaving everything . . . um . . . Casa, lands, whatever is on or under the earth there . . . to his dear friend Thaddeus Benson . . . Who's Benson?" he shot at Mark.

"My uncle."

"Where is he? He's the one to go after this."

"He's dead. He left it to me. I just found it."

"Does anyone else know about this will?"

Mark thought the question odd and nodded. Watching the two men anxiously he saw them glance at one another.

"As I said, it is fortunate you came to me," the lawyer

39

took up smoothly. "Captain Lamson will shortly be going to Cuba. Is the estate of any size?"

Mark squirmed. "I don't know. Uncle Thad said it was."

Lamson was muttering to himself, his finger moving along the black lines. "Here's the word for jewels, Adam. They go to nephews, with—er—lands, houses, gold plate, slaves. It's a perfectly valid will, far as I can see. Would stand in court. And Benson never took it to court . . . mmmm." Again the brown and pale blue eyes met.

Shuttleworth shifted his bulk toward Mark. "Well, my boy, Captain Lamson can act as deputy for you, and for me as your lawyer. He will find the proper proceedings for you and report back."

"But his expenses. How will he be paid?" asked Mark anxiously.

"As is customary," the voice grew more and more smooth. "I will receive one half of the proceeds from your estate, and out of that I will pay the good Captain."

"If that is customary . . ." Mark began.

"More than customary, generous. The larger the estate the more expert knowledge it demands. So, since you agree . . ."

Mark looked at the two men. Both were leaning over the will as though it and all it represented was already in their possession. The musty odor of the small office filled his nostrils.

He rose. "You've . . . been very kind," he said loudly. "I will report to the others. If we agree I will come back." He reached toward the will. Captain Lamson spread his right hand flat on the paper.

"Of course all must be satisfied," Shuttleworth said hastily. "Talk with them. Leave the will here, then, and

40

when you return we will have a fair copy in English for you to keep."

"No." Mark's jaw set. "I'll take it with me."

"But the Captain may sail immediately. If you delay the opportunity will be lost."

"No." Mark said again. "I'll take it. They're waiting," he added quickly, as he drew the parchment to him. For a moment it resisted, held by the flat hand, then it came easily. Mark folded it and put it back in the packet. He could feel the two pairs of eyes following every movement. "Thank you for your help and advice."

Lamson was frowning thoughtfully, but Shuttleworth's fat cheeks creased into a smile. "Not at all. Not at all, my boy. What a lawyer's for. But, remember, there's no one else in the city who knows Spanish, and is going to Cuba, and could be so able a deputy as the Captain here. We'll look for you tomorrow to make the final arrangements."

Mark bowed and marched out the door. Behind him the Captain's voice said softly, "You fool, we would need that will . . ." and was cut off.

On the stairs Mark paused. He could not very well get the packet back in his belt because he had buttoned his coat. Instead he put the packet in the pocket in the tail of his coat, for that had a button, where it would be safe until he could reach his barracks. He was frowning as he reached the street. He was not at all sure he had done the right thing by staying and talking to those two men. He would tell Simon and see what he thought.

On the street he turned left. He would find a tavern and spend tuppence on beer and bread and then be back at the landing in good time. The sun was low and shadows were lying on one side of the street. He crossed a street, glimpsed no tavern, and kept doggedly ahead. The town was only a mile long and half a mile wide, he'd come to one soon. He kept thinking of the two men in the dusty room, and the more he thought the more he felt he had been unwise. There were no people on the street, for, he found, he was nearing some warehouses.

"That's him," called a voice behind. "Quick."

He turned and instinctively backed against a wall as two men, kerchiefs tied across their faces, bore down upon him. One was tall and carried a sword, the other a cudgel. Mark twisted, but the cudgel caught him a glancing blow on the side of the head that knocked him to the ground.

"It's in his belt," he dimly heard. "Get the belt." Rough hands fumbled at the buckle.

"Hold," cried a voice. Running steps echoed on the cobble stones. Above him came a clash of steel.

Mark shook his head and pushed himself from the ground. Two figures were fighting with swords. He shook his head again. The man with the cudgel was circling towards a slender figure in a white and scarlet uniform. As the cudgel raised above the red coat Mark threw himself forward, caught a leg in both hands and jerked. The man fell heavily, rolled, and tried to get up. Mark clung to his leg.

The swords clashed once more and stopped. The man kicked at Mark's head. The next thing he knew someone was lifting him against the wall.

"You're not badly hurt?" asked a clipped, clear voice.

Mark opened his eyes. The white and red uniform was kneeling beside him. "Those men?" he mumbled.

"They ran away." The voice sounded disappointed.

"Can you get up? I think there's a tavern somewhere near."

Mark struggled dizzily to his feet. He started to thank the young man beside him, but decided to wait until they could sit down.

There was a tavern, the Horse and Cart, small and not stylish, two streets away. On one side was a garden with some empty tables under trees. "Beer?" asked the unknown, and disappeared at Mark's nod.

He brought back two mugs and a cambric handkerchief he had dipped in water. Mark wiped his face, brushed his tricorne, shook himself, took a swallow of beer and felt better, though his head hurt. The young man opposite wore the uniform of a British officer, red coat faced with blue, with gold frogging and buttons, white undercoat and stock, narrow sword in a black sheath at his side. His gold-trimmed black tricorne lay on the table. The face above the stock was lightly tanned, with pleasant blue-gray eyes, and looked young beneath the powdered hair. The expression was friendly but wary.

Half rising, Mark held out his hand. "I have to thank you," he said awkwardly.

"And my thanks to you, in turn," said the light voice. "If you had not grabbed that leg I might have joined you on the ground."

Mark grinned at the picture. "But the quarrel was not yours. I am the more in your debt."

"But it was two to one. Not fair, you know. Of course I had to come in on your side." He half bowed in turn. "Cornet Edward Manning, of Lord Whittemore's Regiment, at your service, sir."

Mark knew his bow was clumsy in comparison. "Private

Mark Woodbridge, of the Connecticut Provincials, at your service, sir."

"Really?" The blue eyes looked him over. "I'm glad to know you. You're the first colonial I've met. But I've only been here five days," he added quickly.

Mark drank some more beer. "About the men," he began slowly. "I don't know who they were . . ." But he had an idea, he told himself.

Manning waved a slender hand. "Thieves, no doubt. I've heard they haunt the warehouses. No place to stroll at dusk."

"I was lost. It's the first time I've been in the city."

"Can't find my way around here much better than I can in London, yet. Are you stationed here?"

"No, on Staten Island. I've got to get to the boat, too."

"At the wharf near the fort? My barracks are there, and I can find my way from here, I think. I was exploring the town when I came on you." He gestured as Mark began to unfasten his coat to get at his money. "No. Let me pay, to celebrate our meeting." He raised his mug. "And to another meeting and confusion to our enemies."

On the way through the town they fell into quick easy conversation. They were pleased to find they were both sixteen and both on their first campaign. Manning came from Surrey, and as the second son of his family had always been destined for the army. He had a cousin in the 56th under General Keppel. They both liked to hunt, though Mark had an idea his hunting was of a different sort.

"I'd like to see you again," Mark offered diffidently, as they parted at the fort.

"And I you," Manning answered warmly. "I'd like to learn about your country. Ask for me at the King's Arms, on Broadway, when next you have leave. I'll be there, or watching the races."

They smiled at each other as they shook hands.

It was not until the next morning when they were chopping stove wood for the kitchen fires that Mark had a chance to tell Simon about the interview and its results. Mark stopped while he talked, but Simon kept swinging his regular stroke that split the chunky maple as neatly as a hunting knife slicing cheese. His brown face was impassive as he listened.

"Better start chopping," he advised, when Mark finished, "or that turkey gobbler of a sergeant will be flapping around."

When the pile was stacked by the cooking kettles Simon lead him to a sparse grove of trees and a convenient log.

"There's no use worrying about the buck that got away," he began briskly. "It's not for me to say if you've done right or wrong. You've done what seemed best at the time, and no man can do more. But it does look like it's stirred up some trouble, as the man said when he ran into a hornets' nest. One way that's good. There must have been a good sound to that will or Lamson wouldn't have tried to get it from you, so we know it's not a wild goose chase we're on. One way that's bad, for if they want it enough to knock you out to get it once, they may try another way next time. Thing to do is make it hard for them." He began to sift some of the dry dust between his long fingers, then snapped them.

"Got it. We'll put the papers where they can't get them."

"Where's that?" Mark's head had at last stopped aching and he was feeling better about it all.

"You remember, my lad, it's good to have friends. And there's no friends, as you'll find, like soldiers who've fought together. Take Job Tucker, now. We helped each other out of a mort of skittish spots when we were under Abercrombie. That's why we've both still got our hair. I'd still help Job, and he'll help me."

"Who's Job?"

The round blue eyes looked even more guileless than usual. "He's Old Put's orderly. I got some papers I want to keep safe. I'll make up two packets and Job'll see they get in the bottom of Put's own dispatch box. Won't anyone get them there, until we want them ourselves."

"You've got papers, too?" Mark asked incredulously.

Simon looked hurt. "Any man's got papers, if he's a mind to. You hand over that packet now, and I'll get to Job this afternoon. This way they'll travel to Cuba with us, always be handy, but safe."

"Won't the Colonel find them?"

"Not unless he's a sight more tidy and searching than he used to be. And if he did he wouldn't care. He'd think it kind of cute of us to think of it. He's got brains, and he likes other people to have brains, too."

Convinced, Mark undid his belt, where he had transferred the packet, and handed it to Simon. "Where's the silver dagger?" he asked curiously.

"In a safe place, as the old maid said as she went in the church. It's in my knapsack. People might steal from you, but they know better than to take anything from Simon Etty." He rose and dusted his hands. "We better get back or they'll have a detail after us. Don't worry any more, lad. And the next time you go to town I'm going with you."

5

At the Races
on Bowery Green

It was June fourth when Mark and Simon and Tom Davidson had their next leave. This time the ferry landed them on the East River. Mark tried to act as though he had walked on cobblestone pavings all his life, and was used to city ways, but Tom frankly wished to stop and stare.

Simon prodded him along. "No need to show a city's a new sight to you," he muttered. "New York's no different from New Haven, just got more people."

"Never been to New Haven," Tom pointed out reasonably. "And I never seen the like of this."

"Where're we going?" asked Mark. He kept looking for a boy in an officer's uniform, or for the sign of the King's Arms tavern.

"Tavern's the best place to find what's going on," Simon allowed. "We'll have to spend a penny for beer, but it may be worth it."

Tom and Mark stayed in one corner of the Dog's-Head-in-the-Porridge-Pot (the name had taken Simon's fancy) while Simon moved from group to group and returned, looking solemn.

"They should have told us this was the King's birthday, but I guess they forgot. Someone named Colden's going to make a speech."

"I've heard enough talk from sergeants," Tom said definitely.

"Likewise. Well, there's going to be horse racing on DeLancy's course over near the Bowery this afternoon, and fireworks this evening. Both are free."

Tom brightened. "I'll go to both."

"Put your money in your belt or your inside pocket," Simon advised. "There's more thieves at a race than crows on a new-sown corn field. We'll walk up through the town and over to the track."

They turned into the wide, tree-lined avenue called Broadway that slanted up the island towards the fields and wooded heights beyond Greenwich Village. Now Mark had time to notice that the people looked handsome and healthy, which proved it was not unwise to live in such a crowded place, as one soldier had proclaimed on the ferry. Some of the talk was a queer mixture of English and what Simon said was Dutch, left over from early days. Mark particularly admired that part of Broadway that was so wide it was called The Mall, a pretty street, lined with trees and with flower gardens in front of the neat houses and shops. He would have liked to step into Trinity Church and walk down to admire the massive three-story building that housed King's College, but Tom said he'd had enough of churches and book learning at Granby, but no races there, and it was the races he wanted to see.

Simon knew every sight, and pointed out the tanyards by Collect Pond, though Tom said he'd have known them by his own nose, and Teawater Pump, surrounded by a

group of negro slaves waiting their turn to fill their hogs-
heads with the only water fit for tea on the whole island.
Simon was vague as to when he had been in New York
last, and merely allowed he hadn't taken to the place.
There were too many houses and too many people, and all
too interested in business and too tight with their money.
In Connecticut people were tight, too, he agreed, but a
man had more space and could do as he pleased.

Noticing that Mark looked closely at every red and
white uniform on the street, Simon said, "If you want to
see anyone in this town, either walk on the Mall or go to
the race. And this race is the biggest of the summer. So, if
anyone's looking for anyone, that's the place to look."

"I'd like to see Manning," Mark allowed sheepishly.

"And likely he you. But don't put yourself forward.
Pushing gets people in trouble, as the bear said when he
stuck in the hollow log, and it does more with English
officers than most others. There's all kinds, same as ours,
and get one to forget he's from England and you're a
colonial and you won't find a nicer fellow, if he's nice.
But you can't tell, and you can't count on it, so stand back
until you're asked to step forward."

"I'll remember." The words made Mark uneasy. He
hadn't felt that gulf between him and Manning, but he
could see how it might be there. All his Connecticut pride
rose at the thought of being patronized.

Bowery Lane, a dusty road bordered with two-story,
comfortable houses, orchards, gardens, and meadows with
split rail fences, looked neither city nor country. It was
filled with soldiers and civilians, coaches and horsemen,
all headed toward the open meadow beyond the big, brick,
DeLancy mansion. The dark broadcloth of the merchants'

coats mingled with the red of the English officers, the blue of the Royal Artillery and New York Provincials, the red coats and blue britches of the Royal Americans and the fringed deerskin hunting shirts of the New England Rangers. Mark felt very drab indeed in his sober brown. And nowhere did he see the slim figure of Cornet Manning.

As they drifted from one group to another on the wide meadow they learned that there were to be two races, one long one out to Kingsbridge and back for a purse of twenty pounds; the other, while waiting, would be three times around the mile track of the meadow. The races were obviously between England and her colony, for the officers and backers were obviously divided into two camps and followed by their soldiers and civilians. Simon, unperturbed by the arguments and shouted bets, examined all four horses and then solemnly bet ten shillings on the DeLancy gray with a man who appeared from nowhere with a slate and chalk to enter bets.

"If you're putting ten shillings on that horse, Etty, I'll bet twenty," said a quiet, amused voice behind them.

It was their own Captain Olcott, a teacher from New Haven. Mark gaped. He had not realized the stern, sharp-faced officer, who appeared like an implacable god on Olympus, could sound so friendly. Simon made a half salute, which Mark and Tom copied, and the Captain brushed aside. "If I lose that twenty shillings you can look for three days in the guard house," the Captain added solemnly.

"The gray'll only lose if it's got a bad rider, and from what I hear that isn't the case," vowed Simon. "How about the other race, Captain. Which do you favor?"

They moved to the bay and the black, discussed them in low tones, and made their bets on the English black.

The longer race was started, and the two other horses were being walked up and down, when Mark's eye was caught by a half familiar face. He shifted around behind Simon, circled a clump of soldiers, and stopped. Between an arguing group of Royal Americans and Rangers he could see, in the red-lined blue coat and buff breeches of the New York Provincials, the long figure of Captain Lamson. He was talking earnestly, and was only in profile, but Mark was sure he could not mistake the carroty hair. Then two of the Royals turned to argue with two towering Grenadiers, and Mark saw Lamson's companion. He was an elegant, lean figure, dressed in black, with black hair in a small club. Mark blinked and stepped nearer. Yes, it might be the mysterious Mr. Galvez. Mark's movement had caught Lamson's eye. He looked hard at Mark, tapped Galvez on the shoulder and pointed. As Galvez turned Mark had doubts no longer. The black eyes even at this distance were opaque and hostile. Mark turned away carelessly, as though he had noticed nothing, and edged back beside Captain Olcott.

The shorter race was about to begin. A thickset man in brown climbed on a barrel and pointed out to the two riders where the course lay and that the race was counterclockwise and three times around. Six men with white rags tied to sticks were sent out to mark the course. There was a hush as the horses lined up before a string. From the carriages at the back came laughter and voices; birds were suddenly loud in the trees; from the river floated shouts and clanks of a ship being loaded. Mark had lost all interest in the race. He kept remembering that Simon had said if you wanted to see anyone today you came here. Had those two men come seeking him? He took himself in hand to keep from looking over his shoulder. Then the man on the barrel dropped a handkerchief and the horses sprang forward.

A figure in black appeared in front of Captain Olcott. "You are the officer in charge of this boy?" it asked in soft, accented English. Mark almost sighed in relief now it had happened. Of course it was Galvez.

Captain Olcott moved impatiently. "Yes," he said in the cold voice of the parade ground. Simon slid to a place beside Galvez.

"Then I am fortunate. I have been seeking this person. He stole from me a most important document which I must have as my ship sails this afternoon for the Bahamas."

The Captain looked the man up and down and did not seem to care for what he saw. "Who're you, and what in the name of the Charter Oak are you talking about?"

Galvez gave a slight bow. "Jean LaRoche, interpreter to Lord Whittemore, at your service, Captain."

Mark opened his mouth, but a sharp kick on his shin made him shut it.

Olcott nodded noncommittally. "What's this about a document?"

"He," a white hand pointed at Mark, "knocked me down one evening two weeks ago, and took from my hand a document in Spanish that is of vital importance to me. I saw him clearly, but could not catch him."

Ragged cheers rose from all sides. "First lap completed. The gray's ahead," shouted the man on the barrel.

Olcott looked toward the race and back at Galvez.

"Don't believe a word of it, my good man," he said impatiently.

The black eyes narrowed. "But I can prove it. He carries it in a packet inside his belt."

"What?" For the first time Olcott looked doubtful. "Well, this is no place to prefer charges. Go to headquarters."

"But that gives him time to dispose of it, Captain. And my ship sails in an hour. That is why, when I saw him, I came to you."

Olcott looked irritably at the man, at the dust cloud of the two horses on the far side of the track, and at Mark. "Woodbridge, is there any truth in this?"

"No sir," Mark answered woodenly, and subsided at another kick.

"Make him take off his belt, sir, and then we shall see." The persistence and conviction carried some weight.

Captain Olcott turned to Mark. "It's irregular, but, very well. Woodbridge, give me your belt. We'll settle this here and now."

Mark unbuckled the wide belt and handed it over. The slit for the packet was there, but many soldiers had such a place for their valuables. How wise Simon had been! Olcott passed the belt to Galvez whose eyes had lighted and then filmed with disappointment. "Not a thing there but ten shillings," said Olcott angrily. "See for yourself. Woodbridge, here's your belt. You owe Private Woodbridge an apology, sir."

"No. I am not mistaken. He is just more clever than I thought. But I regret troubling you, Captain." He inclined his head.

"Mark Woodbridge!" exclaimed someone above the

53

growing shouts of "Get new horses." "Speeder up." "Use the whip." Cornet Edward Manning was holding out his hand. Mark grasped it quickly and said "Captain Olcott, Cornet Manning, and Mr. LaRoche, your interpreter."

Edward saluted the Captain punctiliously and looked at LaRoche curiously. The man ignored him. "Captain, my gratitude for your assistance. I shall remember." His eyes flicked over Mark and Simon, and he disappeared in the crowd.

"Captain," said Simon urgently. "Come on. They're on the home stretch. We better watch our shillings."

As they moved away Edward nodded toward the black retreating back. "Who's that?"

"He says he's the official interpreter for Lord Whittemore."

Edward frowned. "I never heard we had any." He looked at Mark curiously. "Is it more of the same?"

Mark nodded. "I'll tell you, sometime."

"Don't need to. I'm on your side, anyway. Let's see the finish."

The finish was spectacular. The American gray was leading when, amid shrieks and cheers and imprecations, the English black nosed ahead in the last ten yards to win by half a length. The crowd settled down to wait for the finish of the long race.

When Simon and Tom joined them, and were introduced, Manning asked hesitantly, "Would, would you join me in a beer at the Bull's Head? It's nearby. The other horses won't be back for an hour."

The brick tavern was surrounded by trees and tables with benches. When the four mugs came Manning lifted his. "To the King," he said, with complete unself-consciousness, and the others drank with him. Then he looked at the three curiously. "You must pardon me," he blurted out, "but as I told Mark, I'm new to the country, and I don't know anything about the colonies, and I haven't met many people."

"We don't get to meet officers, either," observed Simon composedly. "Least not in a friendly way like this."

Manning flushed with pleasure. "I'm the very lowest rank of officer, so I don't really count," he told them ingenuously. "You're all privates? You volunteered?"

"Yup," said Simon, "us and five hundred more from Connecticut. Didn't you?"

"Yes. But you see I'm supposed to. The second son in our family always goes into the army. But I don't understand why you . . ."

"If it's England's fight it's ours," Simon explained, pulling out his pipe and stuffing it. "Stands to reason. She helped us against the Frenchies. Weren't much help at first, but it got better. So it's up to us to help her against the Dons, even if we don't know what it's all about."

"Simon was in the other war," Mark put in. "He's been to sea, too, all around." He liked this pleasant shy lad who was so anxious and eager to understand the new land.

"I know what's troubling you," Simon said suddenly. "Mark, here, is a gentleman, father was before him. Not any money, but gentlefolk. Tom and me, we aren't. But it doesn't bother us, and it doesn't bother Mark. Tom's people have land, but a family's different. Right, Tom?"

"Sure is," Tom agreed cheerfully. "We're farmers. Simon, here's, a rolling stone. Mark's educated and a gent."

"But that doesn't make a difference over here," Simon went on. "We can be friends with anyone we've a mind to in this country. And we're all counted the same in town meeting, if we have forty shillings of property, and we can all stand up and speak our minds. And anyone who doesn't like where he is, can move west, to Pennsylvania, or York State, and take some land from the Indians and set himself up as well as his head and his back'll let him."

"And that makes for a certain independence," Edward grinned. "Go on, please. No one ever told me these things before."

Mark felt that there were a lot of things he'd like to learn from Edward about England, but realized this was not the time or place. From the field across the road there came a sudden shout.

"Drain your mugs," Simon ordered. "Race's coming in."

They reached the line just in time to see the two foam-covered horses race down Bowery Lane neck and neck. At the last moment the DeLancy Black Prince pulled ahead, and the roar that went up could have been heard in Harlem Village five miles away.

Then Edward was swept off by his cousin, a tall, elegant officer. But as he left he said to Mark, "I'll remember you're with Putnam's Provincials, and you remember I'm with the 9th. Perhaps, wherever we're going, we'll be near enough to see each other again."

"I'll remember," Mark promised, and meant it.

"Kind of stiff-like," observed Tom, watching the slim, red-coated figure.

"English always are," Simon allowed. "They're stiff when they don't know you 'cause they don't know if they'll like you or not and can't take a chance. They're stiff when they do know you and like you, for it's not good form to show how you feel and there's always a chance you may not like them as well. And they're stiffest of all when they like you a lot 'cause then they might give way and really show how they feel. Just got to take them like they are. But don't ever think you really know them, for they'll surprise you for sure."

There was bear baiting back in town, and fireworks in the dusk on the Bowling Green. It was only on the ferry boat back to Staten Island that Mark and Simon had a chance to speak together.

"That was right smart of Galvez," Simon began abruptly, "to try to catch you out like that. He probably was leaving today, and saw a chance and took it, as the boy said as he ran off with the pie."

"It's thanks to you there wasn't any pie for Galvez to get," broke in Mark. "It was Galvez, you know, no matter what he said."

"He just made up that name right then. I saw his eyes flicker as he said the name. But just to be sure I got this." He opened his hand: in the light from the whale oil lamp on the bow Mark could see a small silver button carved with the dagger and the scroll. "Cut it off his sleeve," said Simon complacently. "He didn't notice. It's sure proof. We'll be seeing him again, I don't doubt, when we get to Cuba."

6

The Ship
and
the Reef

No leaves were granted during the next six days. On June tenth the four transports bearing Putnam's Provincials, with a Rhode Island company added to crowd the ships still further, so that each soldier was allotted just five feet by two of space, moved slowly down New York bay. A following wind pushed the ungainly ships past the green Jersey shore. The men were massed on deck, glad for any excuse to avoid the darkness and odors below.

"Here come the other transports," said a man beside Mark.

"That point's Sandy Hook," volunteered a man behind. "Been talking of putting up a light there eight, nine years, but no one's done it yet. Had a brother who went aground there, once."

"Must have been the same kind of sailor you are," jeered someone.

"He got off," said the man imperturbably.

The sight of the eighteen ships under their white sails, the soft blue of the sky, the sparkling water hissing along the side, all lifted Mark's spirits. Now he was really off for

Cuba, to a new land, new sights, and whatever lay ahead at the Casa Hermosa. The deck lifted under his feet and settled in a long slide, and his stomach lifted and settled in unison. He looked around uneasily.

"What're those ships stopping for?" someone asked.

"They're all stopping," shouted a man by the rail.

There came a slap and flap of canvas above their heads, the sound of rushing water slowed and vanished.

"We're aground," shouted the man. "Every dang blasted ship's aground."

"Seems there're other sailors like my brother," drawled a pleased voice.

It was backbreaking work to lighten the ship and tug her off the shoal by main force of men and oars, but by late afternoon all the vessels were free of the clutching sand and headed once more to sea. The sun's rim was nearing the flat Jersey shore when the bugle called all men to the deck. The waist of the ship was so packed Mark could scarcely breathe. Above his head the sails had turned a deep gold, and if he bent his head back far enough he could see at the top of the highest mast the red and blue flag fluttering gaily.

"Silence in the ranks," bellowed two sergeants.

Lieutenant Colonel Israel Putnam stepped forward on the poop. For a moment he was silent, as the ship rose, settled, rose. "Men." He paused and raised his voice. "Men. We have been fighting the French since 1756. Three years ago we beat them in Canada, but the war went on. Now Spain has joined France against us. You have volunteered to fight the Spanish. I can now tell you we are going to fight them in Cuba. We're going to help our English brothers capture Havana. That shouldn't take long. Then you'll be coming

59

home, and the Spaniards won't bother England, or us, again."

A cheer faltered to silence as the broad face beneath the black tricorne frowned. "You Connecticut men are under my command. Major General Lyman commands the other provincial troops. But on this ship it is Captain Dawson who commands us all. I expect even better discipline on this ship than on land, and I'll get it. You will drill twice a day, and anyone who complains or does not jump to orders will find himself in the brig. That's all."

Some of the men started to cheer again and stopped.

"Old Put fancies hisself," muttered a man down the line.

"He's all right," said another quickly. "We as served under him knows that. And when he says hop, you hop."

The bow of the ship lifted and came down heavily, as though in agreement.

The voyage south was something to be forgotten as quickly as possible. The soldiers were crowded between decks so tightly they had to lie on their gear in the semi-darkness expect for their two turns at drilling on the main deck. Food was served twice a day. The first day, when Mark found weevils crawling in his two biscuits, he started to lay the biscuits aside in disgust, even though all that remained of supper was a bowl of tepid water called soup. But Simon covered the biscuits with his hand.

"There's a trick to this, like most things, as the farmer said as he twisted the mule's tail. Tap the biscuit hard like on the floor. That scares out the weevils."

"Where do they go?" asked Mark, not caring.

"Back into the next batch of biscuits. But we wear them

out that way. By the last day they're too tired to run, they just curl up and die."

Mark, separated from the small porthole by three rows of men, managed to stoop and knock the biscuit, and did indeed see the weevils crawl out and disappear in Simon's direction.

"Now, no use breaking your teeth, as the oyster said to the mackerel, even if it is on the King's biscuits. Drop them in the soup. That'll make both taste better, though neither will be good."

Though the men had been promised on enlisting that there would always be four pounds of meat each six days, per man, there was only one mouthful every fourth day. The boiled rice was musty and old and had dead ants and moths floating in the sticky mess. At first Mark fished them out; then, like the others, learned to close his eyes and swallow whatever was given him. One pound of sugar was allowed for tea for six men every ten days, and that distribution caused more hard feeling and near-fights than any other event of the voyage. Simon allowed soldiers always grumbled, it was a soldier's right, but these soldiers had more cause than most. But Putnam's discipline held all in line. Later they were to remember that with pride.

As they pushed south the days grew steadily hotter. The tiny allowance of fresh water soon developed a green scum and tasted the way it looked. From the deck they could see the sails of other ships, ahead, behind, to either side, and wondered, as audibly as they dared, if the men had fresh meat and water. Older hands allowed likely not; some ships wouldn't be favored, or lucky, beyond others. Then the ocean turned from gray to deep blue and someone said they were in the Gulf Stream and that meant Cuba wasn't far away. It couldn't be near enough, all agreed.

Except for some rain storms the weather had held fair. On the morning of the twenty-fourth of July the rumor ran around that the next day they would be landing. On deck at sunset Mark strained his eyes, but could see nothing except three transports and a man of war to the east and a flock of sails to the west, white against a gray bank of clouds that was swallowing a red sun.

At midnight the storm struck, and for two hours the ship was tossed like a cork in a shaken bottle of water. It was a relief when the order came to file on deck, fully equipped. When the lines were formed the men were jammed so tightly together no one could raise an arm. The rain was coming down in solid walls of water. The ship pitched so steeply that only the press of bodies kept the ranks upright. The blazes of lightning that cracked up and down the masts showed the officers, clinging to ropes or rails, in a group around the solid figure of Putnam. And always there was the fierce torrent of the wind, bending the bare mast and ever hurling the ship forward into the blackness.

Mark shivered in his soaked uniform. So that was how he came to be here now. Was his quest to end in storm and blackness?

There came a sudden hush in both wind and rain. The ship labored heavily up the slope of a gigantic wave. As she reached the crest a hoarse voice shouted, "Breakers ahead. Breakers ahead."

A quiver ran through the ranks.

"Breakers to starboard. Breakers to starboard."

The ranks stiffened. Mark's breath caught in his throat.

"Need five miles of space to turn this scow," said an easy voice nearby.

"Couldn't turn her then, in this wind."

"Breakers five hundred yards."

The wind came back with a roar and a swoop. The ship lurched down a wave, hesitated, her deck tilted. Laboriously she started upward.

"Tenshun. Dress ranks." The bellow from the poop almost lifted the men from their boots. All straightened.

"There's no wind can outshout Put when he's a mind to be heard," someone said proudly.

"Knock down any man who moves. We're going to hit. Hold ranks."

The wind seemed to pick the ship from the crest of the wave, and hurl her forward. There was a grinding crash at the bow that pushed the lines of men against each other. The ship hesitated. Another wave lifted the transport up and forward. Another crash. The ship halted suddenly, hurling the men toward the stern. A wave poured over the stern, swirled knee high in the waist and out the scuppers as the transport tilted to the left. The ship was firmly aground. Now the sound to listen for was the creaking of timbers as the ship settled more firmly with each wave.

"At ease," called Putnam. "We're stuck on a reef, men. It's an hour to dawn. Come light we'll get out the boats. You'll man the pumps by squads now. Report to me any man who moves except on orders."

So, except for the turns at the pumps, the men stood in ranks. The storm blew eastward, the sky lightened, and suddenly the smothering blackness was gone and everything was gray.

"It's a reef," said someone. "A nice long reef."

"Must have been here for quite a piece," reflected another.

"I didn't come hunting no reefs," observed a man in the rear.

"This one's coral, too. Cuts the feet something fierce."

"I'll take a chance and walk home," piped a new voice.

There was a narrow yellow streak along the eastern horizon as Putnam spoke again. This time his voice carried easily. "We're stuck, men, but not sinking. Shore's just two miles away. Captain Olcott, take the men below. The sailors will get out the boats."

"Might have let us see Cuba before we drownded," growled a man.

"Aren't going to drown for a piece. Ship's steady. She won't break up, neither, with the waves going down."

There came one last terrifying gust of wind which rocked the ship and brought down the mainmast, and then the storm was over. By some miracle no one was hurt when the mast fell, though it wrecked one of the boats in its fall.

Once again the men were ordered on deck, this time to help build rafts. As he struggled on one end of a cross-cut saw that was finding the New Hampshire pine of the mainmast, toughened by thirty years at sea, hard going, Mark looked around. To the right, across blue water, was the low black line that was Cuba. Nearby, empty barrels were being carried from the hold and lashed together, and spare spars and planks were being hammered into rafts. In spite of the haste and bustle the order was perfect, and through it all moved the calm figure of Putnam, directing here, giving a hand to a rope there, until each man felt his Colonel was a partner in each undertaking.

"Pull, dang ye," said Nat Bowen on the other end of the saw.

"Other ships're aground, too," said a corporal, with satisfaction. "I can see two transports *and* a man o'war."

"This one seems solid," gasped Mark, as he pulled back the saw. "Why are we leaving her?"

"Might break up later. Coral reef's no good to a man overboard. Shore's too far to swim to. Old Put's right again."

"He's not old," protested Mark.

"He isn't by years, but he's got more sense than most, and that makes him seem old. Pull, dang ye." And Mark pulled.

The sun was rising as the first two rafts were readied. Sailors climbed down to the waiting boats and settled at the oars, while a raft was tied to the stern of each.

"Company A. Disembark," Putnam ordered, and added, "If you have to swim, men, leave your truck on the raft."

Across the waist of the ship filed the first two squads, each man with rifle, knapsack, canteen, powder horn, cartridge belt. One by one they clambered over the gunwale and down to the rafts to sit in stolid rows. Slowly the boats began to pull the rafts toward the shore.

"Of course there might be Spaniards on the shore waiting for us," Mark observed in what he hoped was a cool voice. The thought had been bothering him for some time.

"The boats will come back if there's trouble," Simon said, "but all looks as peaceful as a church on a Monday morning."

On his own trip ashore Mark could see another transport on the same reef, and two other ships farther away, all immobile, all with flotillas of small boats and rafts heading toward land across the now dazzling water. Ahead of him, behind the line of brown rocks and low cliffs, stretched the green of a forest and distant blue hills.

By afternoon every man from the ship was safely ashore and with supplies for all for three days. There were no Spaniards in sight. A light frigate brought five officers to confer with Putnam and word ran around that next day they would move to the English camp.

The soldiers from the transports had landed on a rocky shore some seventy-five miles east of Havana. Above the shore were thick woods, half scrub pine and oak, half a jungle of dwarf palmetto and stunted palm. Orders came to bivouac on the edge of the forest, to make fires, and to keep on their shoes because of the heavy dew. Even during the supper of inevitable biscuits and soup it seemed to Mark as if the land was heaving and settling gently beneath him and all through the night he felt as though he were still at sea. Simon said that was natural, he'd got his sea legs, now he had to get his land legs back.

By the middle of the next morning the ships that were to move them to the siege were standing offshore. Putnam clambered on a rock and the men crowded around. He looked them over with satisfaction. "You did all right, men. We didn't lose a man on any of the ships." He paused, his stocky figure looking nearly as solid and permanent as the brown rock that held him. "We're moving now to Havana. We're going west of the city, to a place called Chorrera, where Lord Howe has his grenadiers and where the troops from the colonies are camped."

Mark's heart sank. Casa Hermosa was east of the city.

"Seems the biggest problem of this siege is water," Putnam went on. "Too much salt water and not enough fresh. So companies have got to be scattered. Two are staying east of the city. Captain Olcott and Captain Butterworth, you embark last, in the *Mercury*. You'll get your orders from me each day. That's all men. Come on."

Late in the afternoon Captain Olcott's company embarked on the *Mercury*. To the surprise of all they were served immediately a round of rum followed by boiled beef, buttered peas, white biscuits and plum pudding, and tea with plenty of sugar.

"Why didn't we join the navy?" someone broke the contented silence. "Wouldn't get no better'n this at home in New London."

"Do they always feed like this in the navy?" Tom asked.

"Naw. It's just because we got stuck on a rock and they're glad to see us down here. One of the sailors was saying half the army's down sick."

"What with?"

"Fever. Bad water. Hot weather. They're sure glad we got here."

It was the next afternoon before the *Mercury* reached the little Bay of Coximar, east of the harbor of Havana. Great ships of the British line, one the *Namur* of ninety guns, rocked placidly offshore. Frigates, small sloops, barges and long boats scurried up and down along the shore, making a half circle at the rounded point on which reared Morro Castle, the defender of Havana. East of Morro stretched a rocky beach that sloped up to a tree-crowded plateau. There were camps back from the beach, fresh roads slashed upward through the trees to the plateau, and everywhere moved the scarlet and white of the British soldiers. The *Mercury* threaded her way among the ships and dropped anchor at the entrance of a triangle-shaped cove with a small empty redoubt on a low bluff to the right.

From the cove a new road, wide enough for four men to march abreast, lead upward to a plain. Captain Olcott's company turned left, passed a camp where some light infantry were lying under brush shelters, and continued a quarter of a mile to the edge of the woods that bordered the plain. Here was to be their camp. As Mark unslung his knapsack and Simon picked the most likely spot for their own shelter, Mark's one thought was where was the Casa Hermosa and how could he get to it?

7

Water and
a Witch

CAMP, a few tents and many brush huts, was set up as though the siege would last for months. With supper there was only one cup of water for each man, and that had been brought from Chorrera nearly ten miles west, and, Simon said, tasted as if it had walked all the way. For breakfast the next morning there was one cup of tea for each.

Mark had the excuse he wanted. Though it was only eight o'clock the sun was blazing down on the hard reddish earth. Captain Olcott was disconsolately trying to find some shade under four spindly palms.

"Sir," Mark began. "We need water, badly. We're farther west than any other camp. Couldn't Simon Etty and me sort of scout around and see if we could find a well or something that the British didn't go far enough to find?"

Olcott wiped his forehead with the sleeve of his uniform. "Need an almighty lot of water for a company, but anything would help. Sure. You and Etty go ahead. You can have till noon. Look out for guerillas, though. I hear the Spaniards went and gave out arms to the country people and free men and even slaves. Then they got scared and tried to get the arms back and couldn't. Guerillas won't care who they shoot."

The salutes between the two were perfunctory, a mere courteous acknowledgement of bothersome regulations made by distant army men.

Mark and Simon started along the edge of the woods, for even the sparse dry green of the trees gave an illusion of shade. "Sure hope we find some water," observed Simon. "This visit to Cuba's going to be no pleasure jaunt. I never did favor bad water in a hot country. Thought the British'd do better by us than this."

Mark looked at him curiously. "You been here before?"

"Nope, but places like it. Reason half the army's sick is the bad water. But at least there're no snakes to worry about, as the sailor said when he put to sea, and there's nothing much in the way of wild animals. All that's here is wild cattle and alligators they call caymanes, that drag their tails, and we won't meet either on this jaunt."

In spite of the heat it was good to be walking again on solid ground and without the weight of a pack. Bright parakeets fluttered, twittering, among the branches, and the sad moan of mourning doves, that Simon said were too scrawny to eat, filled the air. Then Simon halted and peered beneath a branch at the edge of the wood.

"This looks like a path, and paths go somewhere, and we've seen nothing better."

They had followed the faint trail for five minutes when, ahead, came a low cry, a scuffle, and two rough voices.

"Wouldn't likely be an ambuscade," Simon muttered. "Come on."

He took off at a quick lope. In an open place around a bend were two stocky men in soiled white. One of the

70

men was holding an old woman by her right arm thrust up behind her back. The other man, head thrust forward, was striking her legs with a whip. *"Donde? Donde?"* he was demanding with each vicious cut.

"Cesar," commanded Simon in a loud voice such as Mark had never heard before. A pistol was suddenly in his hand. Mark looked at him in amazement, and then remembered that Simon had said he knew some Spanish.

The men gazed at Simon in astonishment. One released the woman who fell to the ground. Both men raised their hands. They were short and stocky, with broad faces and black eyes and hair.

"Beat it," ordered Simon, and jerked his head down the path.

The one with the whip protested. *"E mala,"* he said, pointing to the woman. *"E bruja. Hay obi."*

Simon gestured again toward the path. Eyes on the pistol, hands still in the air, they started to back away. The one with the whip exploded into unintelligible words. Simon listened, pistol steady, head cocked on one side.

"I don't know what you're saying," he remarked finally, "but whatever it is it probably isn't true. And *lastemar la.*" He pointed to the black heap on the ground. *"Inglesias proteger la."* He raised the pistol. Both men disappeared down the path.

Simon handed the pistol to Mark. "You did wrong, son," he said. "All that time you were watching me and you should have been watching them. Should of pulled out your own pistol, too."

"But it wasn't loaded," protested Mark.

Simon grinned. "Neither was mine. Keep a watch back of us and around us, now, while I see what to do here."

71

He stopped and lifted the woman in his arms. "Where do you live, grandma?"

She opened her eyes and gave Simon and Mark a long unblinking look, pointed ahead on the path, and closed her eyes. Simon strode off, and Mark, feeling somewhat foolish and futile, followed.

A quarter of a mile along the trail and up an abrupt hill brought them to a small hut made of thin slabs of wood held together by dried vines and thickly thatched with palm leaves. A black goat, tethered to a scrub pine, gave a shrill blat. The woman said "*Aqui,*" and Simon set her down on the grass beside the goat. "Hot work," he remarked as he took back the pistol and mopped his face with the other hand.

The woman, the oldest woman Mark had ever seen, and so thin her arms and hands seemed only bones with skin stretched over them, looked from one to the other. Her wrinkled face was very brown and the hair under a black cap was white. "*Inglesias?*" she asked weakly.

"*Norte Americanos,*" Simon told her.

"*Muchas gracias,*" she whispered.

Simon grinned. "*Nada.* If they bother you again let us know." He raised his head and sniffed. "Water, by gum. I smell it. She can do with a drink, too."

The woman moved a hand and pointed down the slope. "*Aqua.*"

At the bottom of the hill they found, beneath a boulder, a good spring of clear water that ran down into a barrel. Mark gave a shudder of pure pleasure as the cold water slid down his throat. It was the first fresh water in weeks and he had forgotten how good cold water could taste.

From his canteen Simon poured a drink for the old

woman into his mug. She drank slowly and handed it back with a crack of a smile that showed she had no teeth. "*Muchas gracias,*" she said more strongly.

"Now for the business of buying water," said Simon, and pulled a sixpence from his pocket. It took a little time for Simon to find out that the spring filled the barrel twenty times a day, and to convince her they would really pay for water and come and fetch it twice a day. But the sixpence proved convincing and at last Simon was sure he had a deal.

"Ask her where the Casa Hermosa is," suggested Mark, at the first pause. "It must be near here."

At the name the wizened face turned and the black eyes looked hard at him. She muttered some words that made Simon shake his head. "It's my guess she doesn't like the place and wants to know why you want to know."

"Tell her because of my uncle," urged Mark. "And ask her if she knows Beltran."

"Uncle. Hmmm, that's *tio,*" Simon muttered. He pointed at Mark. "*Porque Tio,*" he said, and to Mark's surprise the woman nodded and pointed to Mark's face. At "*Conocere Beltran?*" however, all expression fled and she shook her head. Simon shrugged. "Won't tell. But the Casa is back beyond where we turned into the woods. There's a road and we turn right from it. Big white place, she says."

He touched his tricorne. The woman rose with surprising quickness and made a little dip of a curtsey and said something quite clearly. Simon touched his hat again and smiled and Mark followed suit. "She says she is Mama Hanno. She will always be grateful to us and will guard over us," Simon translated. "And she sure understands about the water. Sixpence a day it is, but it'll be worth it."

"Why were the men beating her?" asked Mark as they followed the path back through the wood.

"Something about her knowing where some armed men are hiding in the hills. She has an *obi*, that's something magic, that tells her everything, he said, and he was trying to get it out of her. Couldn't make it all out, though."

As they reached the road Simon looked at the sun. "No time to go exploring. Not wise to overstay leave."

"Let's walk ten minutes," begged Mark. "We should see it then."

"Kind of curious myself," Simon allowed. "Ten minutes."

At the end of the time they had come to the road that turned right. It ran straight through open uneven country towards some woods. Against the woods rose a white wall that stretched beside the road to the woods and at right angles to other woods. A glimpse of red-tiled roofs told nothing of the house below.

"Well, we've seen it and can't do anything about it now, as the farmer said when he saw the ocean," said Simon. "We'll come back later and mosey around."

Mark looked at the wall and wondered what it hid. One thing he must do, he must get inside and find that picture of Don Diego with the unique frame. "Hope there won't be any trouble," he muttered.

"Trouble's for those who go looking for it," advised Simon.

Captain Olcott was inclined to think sixpence a day was a good deal to pay even for ten barrels of water, but after he had taken a drink from Mark's canteen he agreed it was a good idea. So the rest of the day the whole company was

74

busy helping clean out some casks a squad had acquired from the Royal Artillery, and then building dry sleds to drag them, and then hacking a wider path to the spring. There Mama Hanno watched with interest and cackled in a pleased way when Simon told her again that the soldiers would keep anyone from bothering her.

It was the same afternoon, late, that the small boys seeped into the camp. Suddenly, without anyone noticing, seven or eight urchins in short white trousers were edging around the huts, watching the cook fires, wandering from group to group. All the boys were very tanned, barefoot, with black hair and eyes.

"Better nail down your back teeth," growled someone, "or these young devils will take them."

"They aren't taking anything. They're hungry," answered a sergeant. "Here, catch." He tossed a handful of biscuits to three solemn children. The biscuits were caught and disappeared. "See? Hungry."

"I've been hungry since I left Fairfield," said the man behind.

"They've been hungry all their lives," said Nat Bowen. "They all look like picked chickens, and scrawny chickens at that."

Mark had been eating his soup and biscuits when a boy stopped in front of him, looked carefully at his face, and bowed.

"Me, Angel," he said. "Me take care you."

Mark laughed. "You're no angel. And I don't need care taken."

The boy's eyes flashed. "Name Angelo, Angel."

"Where did you learn English?" Mark sopped a biscuit in the soup and saw the boy's eyes drop from his face to the spongy mass. On impulse he held it out on the blade of his knife. The boy took it hesitantly, but it disappeared in one gulp.

"Learn English Casa Hermosa," he answered, when his mouth was clear. "Don Diego," he paused, groping for a word, "had all taught English because his friend English."

"You live Casa Hermosa now?" Mark hoped he sounded casual.

The boy's face closed as had Mama Hanno's. "Not long time. I go now. I come back." And he was gone.

Simon looked at Mark curiously. "Odd, that. But he seems like a good boy."

The next morning, when Mark found his shoes and uniform brushed, he decided Angelo was indeed a good boy. He left half of his four biscuits in a corner of the hut, and, though he did not see Angelo again, the biscuits were gone at noon.

It was another hot humid day. Simon said all the days would be the same, except when there were thunderstorms, which there might be every afternoon until the autumn monsoon. The brush huts were strengthened; the company street straightened and tidied; and some languid drilling was done for an hour. Except for the sentries the men went to sleep.

Mark woke to hear a clipped familiar voice saying, "Cornet Manning of the 9th, sir. Is this Captain Olcott's company? I am looking for Mark Woodbridge."

Mark crawled from the hut, straightened, blinked in the bright sun, and saw Edward Manning, his white breeches and red coat spotless, saluting Captain Olcott punctiliously.

Edward's grin as Mark saluted changed him from an impeccable young officer into a friendly boy. "May Private Woodbridge be relieved of his duties for the afternoon and then mess with us, sir?" he asked Olcott. "I would like to show him our camp."

"Sure," nodded Olcott. "It's too hot for duty." His long face still solemn he looked from Edward to Mark. "Maybe Cornet Manning would like a drink of water," he suggested. "As I hear it, that's one thing this company's got the others don't."

Edward looked polite but incredulous. "Fresh water, here?"

As Mark started for his canteen he almost knocked down Angelo, who was staring at Edward admiringly. "*Amigo?*" he asked in an awed voice.

That was near enough to guess. "Yes, friend, *Inglesias*," Mark threw over his shoulder. The canteen had been buried in the dry ground, and the water was quite tepid, but Edward drank the whole mug, slowly and carefully. "That's the best thing I've tasted since we left New York," he told Mark seriously.

Simon had followed Mark from the hut. "Come back any time with a canteen," he offered expansively. "We'll fill it."

"Cost ha'penny each time," said Olcott flatly, but his eyes twinkled. "Now you've wet your whistle, Cornet, sit down a piece. Perhaps you can tell us some things we'd like to know."

Edward looked at Mark uncertainly, then sat down on a log next to Olcott's. "I don't really know much, sir."

Olcott began to stuff his pipe. Mark, though impatient to be gone, sat on the ground beside Simon. "Old Put didn't tell us much," began Olcott. "Probably he didn't have time and all. But no one else has told us anything, either. I'd

77

like to hear something of what the war's about and what's been happening down here."

"Well," began Edward, obviously a little uncertain how to take this. "As you know, we've been fighting France for six years, and beating her. Last autumn their King, Louis, persuaded his cousin, the King of Spain, to make an alliance with him. Then England and Spain declared war on each other. We have a good navy and Spain doesn't, so it was logical to attack her overseas colonies. And any we can take in the Caribbean here will weaken her resources. We can capture her treasure ships, too. If we have Cuba it will be easier to take Florida and Louisiana. And Cuba's her biggest and most important island, and richest. So here we are to take it."

Olcott nodded. Several men had drifted into a circle around them. "That's good enough for the war. No soldier understands what war's about anyway. What's been going on down here?"

"Really, all I know is hearsay, sir. But, as I understand it from my cousin, our fleet, of about two hundred ships, under Admiral Keppel and his brother, the Earl of Albemarle, reached Havana on June fifth. Our troops landed on the shore, near where you first did, took a redoubt there, and marched inland to the village of Guanamacoa. The Light Infantry under Colonel Guy Carleton—he was with Wolfe and was wounded on the Plains of Abraham, you know—attacked on the right and the Spaniards broke and fled."

"Didn't put up any fight?" asked an incredulous voice.

"They would have if we'd marched to Havana. But there was no use taking the city if we didn't take the forts at the entrance of the harbor, and particularly Castle Morro. It

78

sits right on the edge of a cliff at the entrance, you know, and has a garrison of a thousand men, food for a year they say, batteries of guns, and a ditch seventy feet wide on the land side."

"That's almost as big as Rhode Island bay," jeered a Connecticut voice.

"It's like this." Edward picked up a stick and drew a map on the dust in front of him. "Here's the harbor, big and wide and deep. Here's the city on the west side of the harbor. Here's La Punta, a square castle with four bastions and ditch, at the harbor mouth on the west. Here's Morro, opposite, on the east."

"Where are we?" Mark asked.

"About three miles east of Morro. The coast goes straight."

"What's between us and this Morro?"

"About half of our army." There was pride in Edward's voice. Mark noticed his face and hands were tanned now, his brown, unpowdered hair beginning to bleach. He looked thinner than he had in New York.

"There's a high flat plateau covered with woods called Las Cavannas which extends from back of Morro inland. The hospital's there. The Artillery and Marines are camped along the shore. The other regiments are between them and the Cavannas, or in the Cavannas. The rest of the army is on the coast to the west of La Punta."

"What're we doing about taking Morro?"

"We took their outer batteries on the harbor side. We've built our own battery, but it had to be made out of wood and it burned up before it was finished. We've another almost built. We're mining on the seaward edge of the moat to blow up a bastion. And we've knocked out most of their guns in the fort because ours are better than theirs."

"Where do Albemarle and Keppel hang out?"

"Their Lordships have their headquarters on the ships of the line, the *Namur* and the *Valiant*." The tone was formal.

"Why don't the Spaniards march out of the town and take the army in the rear, on either side of the harbor?"

"They could. Or they could try. But Lord Howe's on a hill west of the city, with his grenadiers on guard, and you," he smiled around the circle, "and the others are on guard here."

There was a moment's silence. Then a voice said, "Now, that's a nicely spoken piece. Amherst himself couldn't have made it clearer."

There were murmurs of agreement and Edward flushed with pleasure.

"Thank you, Mr. Manning," said Olcott. "First time I've known for sure where I was for eight weeks. One thing, though, where'd the mud they call water come from?"

Edward pointed on his map to the western shore. "From a river called Chorrera near where Lord Howe is camped. It's brought to us all in casks by boat. The whole army has to get it from there."

"Tastes old enough to come from the Hudson," muttered Nat.

"And as high as Mount Tom," someone added.

Edward rose and saluted. "May I take Private Woodbridge, sir?"

"Sure. Just do come back, Woodbridge. And, Cornet, come again. You can forget about the ha'pence for water."

"We'll take another lesson any time," Nat called.

Again Edward flushed. "Thank you for listening so patiently."

As Mark followed he heard someone say admiringly, "Must allow that when them English have nice manners they have dang nice manners."

"Too bad more of 'em don't," was the growled answer.

8

Castle
Morro

MARK and Edward followed the dusty road to the dry, rocky bed of the Rio Coximar, crossed on a crude bridge, and a mile further came on a grove of cedars that gave shelter to the tents of the officers of Lord Whittemore's 9th Light Infantry. Once, on the road, Edward had turned and smiled shyly at Mark. "I'm glad things are so informal here," he said hesitantly. "I mean so we can see each other and be friends. It wouldn't do in a formal campaign, you know."

Mark shook his head. "We don't hold with being formal. In Connecticut anyone can be friends with anyone else, no matter who they are."

The brown head nodded. "That does make sense, doesn't it?"

In the center of the plateau lay the tool park and the hospital. Edward shook his head over the hospital. The four surgeons and forty apothecaries were unable to handle the thousands who were sick. Few had been wounded in the fighting, but more than half the army was down with intermittent fevers, putrid ague and fluxes. From there the road led through thick, brushy woods until they came out on the edge of the plateau with a battery on the right.

Dazzled by the sudden brightness of sun on water, Mark blinked, then followed Edward's pointing arm and realized he was at last seeing the ancient, fabulous city of Havana. To his right, along the sloping shore, above brown cliffs, loomed a grim, gray, triangle-shaped fortress that could only be Castle Morro. Opposite him lay a narrow strip of water from which protruded the masts of five ships, which answered his unspoken question as to why the English fleet had not sailed into the harbor and bombarded the town into surrender. Across the harbor entrance squatted the four-bastioned fort, La Punta, and beyond it a low wooded shore. To the left of the fort stretched Havana itself, of a size beyond imagining. Mark could hardly believe that Edward was not bragging when he said London was much bigger. Towers of churches rose above flat roofs, and the heavy square building next to the water, that Edward said was the governor's castle, stood out plainly. It could almost be believed that it was a mile around the walls. Between him and the city lay the half-circle harbor, large enough to hold a hundred fleets.

"Quite a sight," Mark allowed.

"Yes. But of course no one in his right mind would live here. Bad climate, you know." Edward wagged his head solemnly. "Now, let's see how they're getting along with the mine," he suggested, in the manner of a host entertaining his guest. "When they blow it up we'll storm the fort. No one knows yet which regiment will lead the assault. There's a betting pool on it, for all the officers hope it will be their regiment."

"Why?" The thought of rushing that solid, formidable

mass, even through a breech, just did not make sense to Mark, and did make his stomach turn over unpleasantly.

Edward looked at him in surprise. "Only way a soldier can get ahead, get mentioned in dispatches, get promoted, is in a fight. No fighting, no promotions." He looked quite serious. "That's why an army always wants war and not peace."

Mark realized that the army was far more important to Edward than it could be to a volunteer, so he merely said, "I see. Let's go to the mine," and left the attitude toward war as something to think about some other time.

They returned to a branching road which led through woods, across an empty parade ground, and descended to a narrow rocky shore. Here some sappers were at work, partway up the side of the plateau.

"Why put a mine here?" asked Mark. It seemed too far away.

"The ditch is narrower here and it's protected from the fort. Look, almost at the shore, see that narrow wall of rock that was left to keep the water from flooding the ditch? We have to cross on that to get to the rock below the bastion wall to tunnel for the mine. The guns of the fort can't be deflected enough to fire down into the ditch, or on our mines."

"Don't they know what we're doing?"

Edward shrugged. "We don't know. They can't see much. There may of course be spies who could tell them. Probably they think no one could storm across that ditch. Their seaward guns knocked out three of our ships of the line when my Lord Albemarle tried to see if the fort could be reduced by gun fire. The ships lost their masts, and not a dent was made in the walls. So that wasn't tried again."

"Let's go closer."

A group of officers were standing around the entrance of the mine tunnel. Edward pointed out the red trousers and sash of an aide to a general, which looked to Mark almost the same as the Royal Artillery, and the blue breeches and coats of the gunners. Mark glanced seawards. The low sun was turning the sails of the sloops and frigates to vivid gold above the flat blue of the ocean. The north, or sea walls of Morro seemed to gather in and reflect the mass of yellow light poured from the west on water and masonry, making deeper the shadows engulfing the landward walls. Mark shook his head. It was hard to believe that he, Mark Woodbridge, was seeing anything so strange and beautiful.

Strange indeed. The climate must be affecting his eyes, for now he was seeing things. He peered again at the walls that stretched inland from the rocks at the water's edge above the great ditch. He thought he saw a ladder going up the walls from the rocks. He blinked and peered again. It looked like a ladder, anyway. But he would feel better if Edward could see it, too. He pointed.

"Do you see anything there?"

"Well . . ." Edward's glance was bewildered. "Yes. I see the fort and the ocean and the rocks."

That wasn't what Mark wanted. He pointed again. "Do you see anything against the wall? Look quick before it vanishes. I need to know."

"It's just the ladder you're looking at."

Mark nodded vigorously. "So it *is* a ladder. Just a simple ladder?"

"It's four ladders tied together, but they're all simple."

85

Edward grinned. "We put it up there. And a sergeant took a squad up one night to see what could be learned about the state of the defense."

"Just like that? Up the ladder and around the fort?" Mark was sure Edward was pulling his leg.

"Well, he only got part way around the bastion. He did find out there were no soldiers on that lower bastion above the ditch, but then he heard a patrol coming so they all climbed back down again. He was ordered back up to reconnoiter, but by that time the garrison was alerted and daylight was coming so he didn't have to go again after all."

The story was too much. Mark laughed until he choked. "It's as good a tale as one of Simon's," he gasped.

"But it's true," Edward insisted. "Ask anyone."

In the end Mark had to believe the exploit. "Let's go closer," he said again, "just so I can say I saw it when I tell about it."

As the two moved nearer the mine the officers moved closer also. "It'll be a number of days, gentlemen," said one in the plain buff uniform of the Engineers, in a voice tinged with a burr from Scotland. "I can't tell ye better than that, no matter how many times ye may ask."

"But time is getting short, Colonel," put in an older officer with a face like a worried sheep. "We are in late July. The monsoon season may break on us any day, any day, I say. And if a monsoon storm should scatter our fleet, as you may be sure it would, our entire army would be lost. Every man jack of them, Colonel, would be killed or captured in three days. Everything must be done quickly, now."

"We are doing our best, sir," answered the engineer

calmly. "But it takes time to go through solid rock, particularly under the most difficult conditions I have ever encountered."

"But we'll attack here?" asked a faintly familiar voice.

"Aye. But it depends on whether we bring down enow of the walls to fill the ditch."

"Oh, come now, Colonel McKellar. You've got enough dynamite to blow up the whole fort."

The Scotsman did not smile. "E'en if we wanted to do such a thing there would be no room in the sap for such a charge."

"But you've two saps running!"

"Aye, as a wise man carries two pistols."

A prickle went up Mark's spine. Forgetting Edward he edged to one side where he could see more of the group. In the center, talking easily, his attitude formal and quite military, stood Captain Lamson.

Edward tugged Mark's sleeve. "Come away. Not good form to hang around officers."

Backing obediently, Mark still watched the group. The movement must have caught Lamson's eye, for he half turned and looked straight at Mark.

Mark stumbled a little as he followed Edward. Again the sharp eyes had recognized him.

It was night now, the swift tropic nightfall to which Mark could never grow accustomed. The sun had set behind a towering pile of puffy clouds.

The evening meal of the junior officers of Lord Whittemore's regiment was some stringy beef from some cattle that had been rounded up south of Guanamacoa by a squad of cavalry, a mess of something white and pasty called duff, and hot tea strong enough to disguise the taste of the water from Chorrera. The three young officers with whom the two boys ate were polite to Mark, but after one glance at his uniform had nothing further to say to him and talked about fox hunting at home. Mark and Edward discussed in low tones various dogs they had had. The meal took only ten minutes, and as Mark was loth to return so soon to his own encampment the two strolled towards the shore, moving from pools of firelight through pools of darkness between. Once Mark thought he saw a figure strolling in the same direction, but lost it beyond a fire of the Royal Artillery.

They came out near the rock wall that led to the cliff below El Morro. There was still enough starlight to the east to see the high white combers with their glints of phosphorescence, and in spite of his weeks on the water Mark found he could still enjoy watching the waves reach a crest, the line of frothy white run along as the crest curled, and the sudden pitch forward and roaring crash of the tumbling water. Somewhere behind them a stone rattled.

"Someone's over by the rock curtain," said Edward. "Perhaps another reconnoitering party's going up the ladder."

Mark shivered at the thought. From the black clouds mounting the sky came a low rumble.

"We better see who it is," Edward insisted. Mark followed him blindly from the shore over the rocks toward the big moat. He could hear no sound but their own stumbling progress. Then Edward halted. Their eyes now accustomed to the dark, they could discern a figure moving slowly across the curtain and turning towards the ladder.

"Come on," muttered Edward. "One man has no business going up those ladders."

"Neither have two," said Mark to himself, but he followed. The rock curtain was wide enough for one person. Mark edged forward, not daring to look down on either side. Once on the solid rock of the cliff he sighed with relief. Perhaps Edward would stop this foolishness now. Through the darkness he could feel as a tangible presence the formidable blackness of the cliff and the fort looming above him. This was no place to approach lightly. But he found himself following Edward to the ladder. As he put his hand on the stout wood, he felt a faint tremor from above. Someone was indeed climbing. He peered upward, and a flicker of lightning showed an officer in a uniform that was not red and white.

"I'm going after him," Edward whispered.

"Why?" asked Mark reasonably.

A flash of lightning, still distant, showed a suddenly new Edward. His eyes were dancing, and a broad grin of delight made him look like a small boy about to climb a neighbor's apple tree after forbidden fruit.

"Think what a ploy it would be," he said hurriedly, "to get up and down that ladder."

"We might not get down," Mark pointed out, "and if we did we couldn't tell."

"Oh, we'll get down." The voice was laughing and assured. "And even if we couldn't tell, we'd know ourselves, inside, that we'd done it, and what a joke it would be on those who didn't dare. Besides, it's my duty as an officer to investigate any strange occurrence."

"All right. I'll come," Mark agreed reluctantly. "But I

don't like it." He spoke to the wind, for Edward was already mounting the ladder.

It was a long and terrifying climb. The wind was growing stronger, pushing him sideways as his fingers groped for the next rung. Though it was firmly fastened below and, apparently, tied above, the ladder swayed a little at every step. Mark could not keep his mind from the black rocks below as he forced himself to watch for Edward's dim figure just above. Then Edward disappeared and his fingers were scraping on cold stone. The parapet was wide, and he had to throw himself forward and over it, and then he was standing on the inside of Morro's walls.

In his absorption in climbing he had not noticed the thunder, but now lightning flashed more brightly. He saw Edward and the wide *chemin de ronde* that edged the wide triangle of the bastion and a narrow passage at the end of the right-hand wall. No Spaniard was in sight.

"We better make for that passageway," said Edward softly. "Perhaps we can see more from there."

Feeling confident on the welcome smoothness of the stones, they tiptoed through the passage and halted, uncertainly. There was a feeling of space before them and Mark realized the whole of the fortress lay ahead. Backs to the wall, they waited for the next lightning flash. Impatiently, Mark poked his head around the corner, and drew it back sharply. Soft footsteps halted just beyond.

"All right, if you won't believe me you won't," said a familiar voice. "I tell you they do have a sap by the rock curtain and another above the ditch. They'll blow them up and your precious wall at the same time."

There was no mistaking the voice. Mark was surprised at recognizing the man they had followed.

There was a low reply.

"Why would I climb that blasted ladder if it weren't true? I admit it solved my problem of getting word to you and earning my pay. Your agent in New York gave me a quarter of the money. Now I've earned the rest. I was to tell you the English plans and get enough money to stay out of jail—not to see you make use of what I brought you. But you can land a squad and destroy the saps any night before they know it, if you want to."

In the silence that followed Mark was aware that the wind had suddenly dropped. Thunder crashed, nearer.

"*Adios*," said Lamson. "I'll expect the money."

Mark and Edward flattened against the wall of the passage. His steps passed them and crossed the *chemin de ronde*. And then a flare of lightning lighted the fort. A figure at the end of the passage gave a startled shout. Lamson flashed around.

"What?" he called, and the light was gone.

Mark started toward the man. He was a spy; he must not get back to camp. A strong hand gripped his shoulder. "Who are you? You're young and English; I could see that. Get down that ladder. That imbecile may be stupid enough to rouse the fort." The hands propelled the boys to the parapet. "It's here. Climb down. I'll follow."

Mark's groping hands found the ends of the ladder. He turned, squirmed over the parapet, felt the rung, and started down. Edward was protesting something. And then the heavens opened and rain descended in sheets. Blinded, clinging desperately to the now slippery rungs, Mark edged downward. The ladder trembled and swayed from the triple weight. He shut his eyes so if lightning came he could not see the black rocks waiting beneath him.

At the bottom of the ladder he sat down quickly. Edward stood beside him, but Mark could feel that he also was shaking. The ladder gave a final creak.

"Now, you two young fools, who are you?" The voice was commanding, but more amused than hostile.

Mark tried to stop Edward from giving their names, but it was too late.

"What took you up there? You could have been killed."

"We saw you and followed," Edward told him steadily through the downpour.

"Oh, so that's it."

"And we heard . . ." Mark added hotly.

"You did . . . ? What's that name again? Woodbridge? I'll be blowed. Our paths do cross."

Abruptly the rain was slackening. Mark shivered in the sudden coolness that followed. The thunder was rumbling away to the east.

"Suppose we make an agreement, then?" Lamson spoke easily but firmly. "I'll say nothing about you, and you say nothing about me."

"No," Edward said. "We heard you tell about the sap."

"Then you heard that the idiot did not believe me and would do nothing. He wouldn't even promise to tell the commander, in spite of the money they'd paid for word of the English plans. But there's no harm coming to the saps from those in the fort. They'll do nothing about it. And they couldn't come around the point from the city and attack because of our fleet. So no harm's done."

"No," said Edward again.

"Look here. Be sensible. Who'll believe you? It'll be my word against you and this young provincial. You'd be laughed at by the whole army. A likely tale you'd have against a captain. Furthermore, I've just messed with the Royal Artillery. They're so busy arguing about horses they'll never know I've been gone half an hour, and my orderly is there to say I never left the fire. Do you see?"

"Well . . ." Edward was wavering.

"All you'd do with your tale would be to make it awkward for the three of us—get us locked up for a few days on one of those ships out there. And I'd get out first. No one would believe you against me."

The thought of the darkness of the hulks on the ships, the smell and the constant tossing was too much for Mark. "He's right, Edward," he said in a low voice. "He'd win out. They wouldn't believe us. We've no proof. We'd better agree."

"Sensible, as a true Yankee," approved Lamson. "Besides, young Woodbridge, I don't want anything to happen to you. We'll have a talk soon."

"All right." Edward's voice shook a little. "I'll agree, too."

"Good. Know I can trust an English officer's word. It's too bad we can't get the praise we deserve for that trip up and down." Lamson was amused now. "Start for your camps. I'll wait here."

As they turned there was a sudden splintering crash behind them.

"It's the ladder," cried Edward sadly.

"They must have found it at last." Lamson's voice floated to them through the darkness. "That sets the seal on our bargain."

"Yes," Edward agreed. "Even if we could tell, no one

would believe us now. But," his voice brightened, "I told you we'd get down again, Mark. We did it. We can always remember that."

The clouds had rolled away and the starlight guided them vaguely back to the Lord Whittemore's and the road to Coximar. The two did not speak. Too many might hear. On the road Edward said, "Thanks for coming with me. I'll see you as soon as I can get away."

"I couldn't let you go up that ladder alone," Mark said awkwardly. "And . . . and thanks for the supper."

It was a lonely, wet, muddy walk back to the brush shelter. On the way he thought about Edward and how surprising he was and how hard it was to know what went on inside his head. And he thought about Lamson and the will and Casa Hermosa and the portrait of Don Diego.

9

A Rescue
from
Casa Hermosa

MARK went to sleep thinking of Casa Hermosa, and woke filled with determination to go there that day. Simon, when he heard about Captain Lamson, had agreed that the sooner Mark got to the picture frame the better. But they could not talk about it at breakfast for Angelo appeared, and this time they shared their tea and biscuits happily. Some dozen of the small boys had been accepted by the Connecticut men. The children made themselves useful and brought in odd vegetables and fish for the stews, which were allowed because nothing could make stews taste worse, and sometimes they actually tasted better.

"Where you live, Angelo?" Mark asked idly. He was coming to like the thin bright boy with the half-Indian, half-Spanish features.

Angelo waved a thin hand. "Village. Family long time live Casa Hermosa. Now only brother there." His English was improving.

"Did you like the people there?" Simon asked cautiously.

"Family like Don Diego, yes. Nephews, men now, no."

"Ever hear of a man named Beltran?"

Angelo ducked his head. "Know name. Long time go in hills."

"Why'd you come talk to me the first time?" Mark was shying away from the name, he'd asked about it twice now, and that was enough.

The brown eyes looked up at him in surprise. "You not know? Mama Hanno tell me look for boy, not man, hair brown, eyes gray," he fell into a singsong as though repeating a lesson, "shoulders broad, tall, not too tall, wide face, kind look."

Mark felt himself blushing. "But why me?"

"You help her. She help you. *Señor* Simon no need help." He grinned impishly. "Also boys know all happen. Mama Hanno like know. So I help her too."

Simon chuckled. "He had you sized up pretty well, Mark, as the peddler said as he pushed the shoat into his pack. But it's nice of Mama Hanno to want Angelo with you," he added hastily.

"Mama Hanno wise," asserted Angelo solemnly. "How you say—know all things. Has *obi* tell her. Know all people. Bad men say *bruja*. No *bruja*, just know more."

"That's why the men were after her that morning," Simon put in.

"*Si, si*. They try find out where men in hills." He looked quickly over his shoulder and back. "Men in hills. Men run away from Casa Hermosa, other *casas*, when beaten too much. Hide. Can't find. But Mama Hanno know. She their friend. Tell them things need know."

Languidly a bugle blew assembly. Angelo scooped up the wooden bowls to scrub clean with sand and leaves.

While they were on wood-gathering detail Simon took Mark aside. "Know you're itching to go to Thad's place.

But don't go in alone, as the bride said to the groom at the church door. We'll get to go this afternoon."

But that afternoon Simon was sent inland with a squad to find cattle or any food the Spaniards or English had not taken. Mark was lying in the hut, wondering if he dared ignore Simon's advice, when Edward poked his head in the low doorway.

"See?" he said cheerfully. "I came soon. It is dull at the 9th for there are none my age, and there is nothing to do."

Mark crawled outside. "Are you game for a walk? It's about four miles."

"With a drink of your good water I could walk any-where," Edward grinned, "if I can have another drink when I come back."

Captain Olcott seemed inclined to draw Edward into a discussion of the war and its merits, and then of the differences between schooling in England and New Haven, but decided it was too hot to talk and waved them away. Most of the soldiers were still asleep in their huts, and the sentry merely blinked and returned to his doze. The heat was a smothering blanket, but it was no hotter moving than being still.

Out of sight of the camp Mark stopped. "Let's take off our coats."

Edward was shocked. " 'Gainst regulations. Full uniforms always."

Mark was shrugging off the long black, square-cut coat. "Don't care. No one'll see us. We can put them on before we get there."

"I can see why colonials are an influence for freedom." Edward began to undo the gold buttons. "But be sure I have it on in time or it means confinement to quarters."

He shuddered at the thought as he draped the red coat over one arm. His white shirt was fine cambric, and clean. He carried no side arms.

"How do you keep so clean?" Mark asked curiously. "We can't."

"One of the advantages of being any kind of an officer. My Bates takes care of everything. Heavens, I couldn't do it myself." He glanced down at his gaiters, freshly clayed and immaculate. "I must say I feel sorry for our soldiers. They have to keep everything they wear spotless, and it takes most of their time."

Mark had known inside he was going to tell Edward his story. He had to tell someone, and he could trust this friend. So, as they tramped the hard-packed road, he poured out the tale of Uncle Thad and his will and letter and death, and the encounters with Lamson and Galvez. Edward was a good listener; he never interrupted or showed surprise. But when the story was over he stopped and looked seriously at Mark.

"You know, I believe it all. Most people wouldn't. It's like a fairy tale a nurse tells. But what do we do next?"

Mark's heart warmed at the "we." "I want to get in the Casa and get that picture of Don Diego. I've got to have time to go over the frame. I don't know how the message is hidden."

At the crossroads Edward put on his coat. "It is a military maxim never to reveal your strength or purpose," he began. "We'll stroll up as if we were visitors. Or we can be looking for provisions. That'll give us a good excuse."

"Then what?" asked Mark doubtfully, as he buttoned his own coat.

"Then we'll see what happens. We improvise. A good

general, like Marlborough, always keeps flexible. If we can't get in we'll retire to our positions and figure out another attack."

"I'm glad you're along," Mark told him sincerely.

"So am I. This is much better than listening to the officers talk about their campaigns, or hunting in the shires, or about London. Besides, we must see that justice is done."

The white wall of the Casa Hermosa proved to be flaking and dirty, and the high, wrought iron gates were rusty and ajar. The driveway was bordered with towering palms, but what had once been grassy lawns was baked clay, filled with stumps where trees had been cut down, empty pools, and pock-marked with holes as though someone had been digging. The house at the end of the drive was white, with high grilled windows and treetops in the distance. There was no sign of life.

"Come on," said Edward. "Look military but at ease."

Mark laughed. "You look military, I'll be the at ease."

They strode purposefully up the straight drive until they reached an arched gateway barred by a grill.

"It's a tunnel that goes through the house," exclaimed Mark. "There's a garden, or something, beyond."

"That's a patio. Most Spanish houses are built around an inner courtyard like that, for coolness and privacy."

"*Señores?*" said a heavy voice in front of them.

A thickset man with stringy black hair and small eyes, in dirty white shirt and trousers, had appeared on the opposite side of the grill. His skin was so oily it looked as if it oozed grease instead of honest sweat. In his right hand he held a whip. Mark was almost sure he was one of the two men he and Simon had found with Mama Hanno. The expressionless eyes flickered from one to another.

99

"*Solados*," rapped Edward. "From the army. We examine the house."

"But there is nothing here, *Señores*," whined the man. "People, food, there is nothing."

From behind him came a faint cry of protest.

"We will see that for ourselves." Mark marveled at the tone of command that seemed so natural to Edward. He couldn't have sounded like that, he knew. "We will come in." Edward pushed open the grill.

As they stepped into the arched tunnel the man moved quickly to stand between them and the patio beyond. On either wall loomed tall double doors. "Open that," said Edward pointing to the left.

Beyond the heavy door was a long high room with tiled floor and beamed ceiling, dim because of the jalousies at the windows. At the far end was a fireplace and above it a portrait of a lady in a white dress. Edward looked around quickly, at the long black table in the center, the massive armchairs that marched down both walls. "All right. Nothing here. The other room," he ordered.

Crossing to the opposite door Mark was sure he heard another quick protest.

"*La Sala Grande*," muttered the man as he pushed back one door.

This appeared to be the same size as the other. The tile floor was reddish through the dust and the ceiling beams were painted in blue and gold. The walls showed large oblong spaces of lighter color, and there was a similar empty space above the fireplace.

"What was there?" asked Edward, nodding toward the walls.

"But tapestries, *Señores*, and there, over the fire, a

magnifico portrait of Don Diego Peneranda." The man was now obsequious.

"What happened to them?"

"All taken by the *Señor* Pedro to the Casa Alta in the hills to the south for safe keeping from the *Inglesias*. There is nothing here, *Señores*."

Mark's heart sank. The picture somewhere in the hills! Now he never would be able to get it.

Edward insisted on marching through the huge dusty kitchen and store rooms, though they were indeed empty. But through an open door Mark had seen something white move in the patio. Quickly he strode into the courtyard, where dusty, dying palms and twisted fig trees were surrounded by parched bushes. In the center a cracked pool held a leaning statue of a lady with a pitcher, which had not poured water for a long time.

"There is nothing there," shouted the man behind him.

But Mark had again heard the cry of protest. He followed a broken tile path toward a distant corner. There were two figures ahead. One was kneeling on the cracked paving beside a small gray donkey. The other figure held a meat cleaver and was motioning the first aside. Edward strode forward quickly. "Here, what's this?" he demanded.

The kneeling figure was a thin, ragged young man with a drawn desperate face. He pointed to the donkey's leg and then to the standing man. Edward dropped down on one knee and gently began to feel the leg. The donkey quivered all over but lay still. Mark glanced at the fat man who was scowling at the others, at Edward, at the donkey; one hand was stealing towards the fat man's belt.

Mark tapped him on the shoulder. "No," he warned.

The man waved his hands quickly in front of him as

though to show they were empty. "It is *nada* for the *señores* to trouble. The burro has broken a leg. Can't walk. We will kill and eat. Roberto *stupido*."

"*No es verdad*," the young man panted, his hands clasped beseechingly. "*Burro di mia madre*. They take it, beat, now kill. We need."

"No reason to kill the little beast," said Edward cheerfully. "We can set this leg, put on a splint, and in six weeks it will be fine again. Mark, you find me some flat sticks and two longer ones. Send those men away. Their faces might put me off. No, wait, we'll need some bandages. If they won't give you cloths, take their shirts."

Reluctantly the fat man produced a dirty shirt and then the two retreated to the kitchen. "Don't move," Mark ordered, "or all *soldado* come here . . ." He made a motion of shooting.

By now the shirt was torn in strips and the sticks laid by Edward's hand. Mark could only produce objects as directed as he watched Edward gently feel the ends of the bones and bring them swiftly together. After that the splint was simple. The longer sticks were to enable the beast to hobble.

"He'll be all right," Edward said, dusting his hands. "Roberto, don't let him walk much and feed him up."

The burro was helped to its feet by an overwhelmed Roberto and leaned trustingly against Edward. Mark saw the slender fingers rubbing gently behind the ears.

"*Muchas gracias, Señores, muchas gracias*," stammered Roberto, "*y di mia madre*."

"That's all right," Edward assured him awkwardly. "But don't leave it here." He glanced around the dusty patio.

"I take to Mama Hanno," said Roberto in a low voice. "Burro safe there. She cure."

Steadying the limping burro the three walked slowly out of the Casa and down the palm-lined avenue to the gate.

"Where'd you learn to take care of animals?" Mark asked curiously on the road back.

"Why, at the home farm," Edward told him. "Never could bear to see animals in pain. So I picked up all I could from the men. Before I left for the army I could take care of all our dogs for almost everything," he added proudly.

Mark shook his head. "You English will always surprise me. You better brush the dust off your trousers."

Dismayed, Edward halted and brushed furiously. "We don't need to say anything to anyone," he suggested.

"No. We better not say anything about any part of our visit."

Edward looked sideways. "I'm sorry about the picture not being there. Perhaps when we take Havana and the island surrenders you can get to that place in the hills. That's the best thing I can think of now."

"Guess you're right," agreed Mark disconsolately. "But all that may take more time than we have."

10

The Fight
at Peralta

BUT the more he thought about it, after Edward left, the more he was sure his friend was wrong. There was no knowing when Havana would be taken. Captain Lamson might find some way to get in touch again with Galvez with the news Mark was in the army and would be seeking his inheritance. What the two could do he could not guess. They could not know what he knew, but Galvez certainly would not wish Uncle Thad's inheritor on the island when it was captured. With the picture and its frame gone, he had no clue as to where the Peneranda hoard was hidden. Even if he could not reclaim all Uncle Thad's legacy he could at least take the jewels, if he could find them. But Casa Alta was in the hills with the land between filled with guerilla bands and Spanish troops.

He shoved the problem to the back of his mind when he found that the foraging party had returned with two lean cows which were already butchered and readying for the pot.

"We paid for them, too," Tom Davidson told Mark proudly. "Ten good silver shillings each. They were hidden in a wood and the woman didn't want to let us have them. Said the Spanish soldiers would be mad, near as we could figure out. We told her we needed them more than the Spaniards."

"I kinda felt sorry for those folks," allowed Nat Bowen. "Look like they have done nothing but work all their lives and never had a full meal. And the places they live . . . not so good as my chicken coop."

"*Vaca* of *Serafina*," said Angelo in a low voice, pointing to the iron kettle. "She buy new vaca when war done. Soldiers took her man work on city walls. He never come back."

"See?" said Nat. "Those folks'll be better off when we get the Spanish out of here."

Even though the meat had to be eaten in two days on account of the heat, the spirits of the company rose considerably by the time the cows had been consumed.

It was late the next afternoon that Angelo panted up to where Mark was mending a tear in his coat while Simon whittled. The boy flung himself down on his knees before them, his hands clasped, his brown eyes filled with tears. "*Ay de mi*," he sobbed. "*Ay de mi. Señor Mark.* Come help us. The soldiers. They come to village. They say kill us all because we help *Inglesias*, give *vacas*. One village burn now." Then he covered his face with his hands.

Simon leaned forward and patted him on the shoulder. "All right, sonny. We'll help. Calm down."

Angelo rubbed his hands in his eyes and straightened. "I calm now, *Señor*," he said with a pitiful dignity. "We send for men from *montañas*, but afraid they no come soon. So I come to you."

Simon got to his feet. "Quite right. Come, we'll talk to Captain Olcott."

The Captain listened, rubbing his knuckles up and down his right cheek. "Do you think it's straight, Simon?" he asked.

"Don't doubt it, sir. Angelo's a good boy; he's mighty upset."

"Sounds just like those Spanish," muttered Nat, who had drifted over.

"We haven't done any fighting," muttered Olcott, as though thinking out loud. "And we came to fight. May not get any for a long time, either."

"And if it's on account of those cows we took, why we're honor bound not to let them folks get hurt," Nat went on.

"You're right," Olcott agreed. "It's our duty to protect those who helped us."

"What'll Old Put say if we high-tail off to a fight on our own?" asked a newcomer.

"No time to ask him now," the Captain drawled.

"He'll just be mad he wasn't along," vowed Simon positively.

"We can't go officially, like a company," snapped Olcott. "But volunteers, now . . . Simon, Nat, you go see who wants to volunteer, and any who don't want to can go join the Rhode Islanders."

By the time the men had gathered their gear and guns four other boys had joined Angelo in the company street, their faces pinched with anxiety but making no sound as they waited. The company fell into two lines, with the Captain and the men who had been on the foraging party in front.

106

Angelo stepped beside Olcott. "We show shortest way village," he offered.

"Right, sonny. But," he turned to the men behind him, "did those cows come from the village?"

"Nope," Nat answered. "They come from a mighty poor looking place down the road toward the city."

Olcott swung around. "Where the soldiers coming from, boy?"

"From Havana. They in next village now."

"Then, Nat, you take ten men. Go ahead down to that place. If the Spanish are mad about the cows we ought to get to that place first. You look out for those people until we get there."

"*Enrico!*" Angelo called shrilly. "*Estos hombres, hasta, Serafina.*" A small boy slid beside Nat. "He knows short path Serafina," Angelo explained.

A hundred yards beyond the camp Enrico, followed by Nat and his men, turned into the woods; the rest followed Angelo and Olcott down the road to turn off to the right within a mile onto a mule track across barren ground, through sparse woods, and up a long rolling hill to dip down into a shallow valley beyond. They began to pass huts, poor things built of strips of palm wood bound together and roofed with palm leaves, or solid cubes of mud without windows and an open space only for a door. There were no people, not even a dog to bark or a hen to cackle. The men made clucking sounds of sympathy over the huts. And around a low hummock they came on the village of Peralta.

It was only a collection of sagging or crumbling huts huddled around a small open square. In the center of the plaza rose a wide-spreading tree, the only green thing in sight. At the left end was a low church, once white-washed, now stained and dirty with open, sagging doors. On the top of the three steps stood a small figure in black, gesturing and calling to the women and children who were crowding toward him, shoving those nearest into the church and waving on the laggards. From the road that led to the right, eastward to the bay and the city, rose a languid cloud of black smoke. From a distance came four shots.

"Who's that at the church?" asked someone.

"The village priest," answered Olcott. "He's trying to get them all into the church. And I've heard that the Spanish burn churches when they're full of women and children." There was a shocked silence. "But they won't burn this one," he added, and the group sighed with relief.

They moved toward the church. The priest cast one glance at them and began to call urgently, "*Inglesias. Prisan.*"

"You don't have to be afraid of us, sir," Olcott told him gently, taking off his hat. "We'll take care of you." But the priest gave him a hunted glare and crowded in the last of the women.

Two small boys raced down the plaza yelling at Angelo. Mark saw the priest was listening, then turned and tried to close the doors. When he found he could not, he placed himself in front of them with his arms folded. A shepherd looking after his flock, thought Mark.

Angelo was reporting to Olcott and Simon. "Boys say soldiers coming on road."

Olcott rubbed his cheek. "Ask him, Simon, if the Spanish know we're here."

Simon spoke enough for Angelo to shake his head violently.

"Nice," observed Olcott thoughtfully. "How many?"

"Boys don't know sir, just say thousands."

"Hmmm. All right. Columns divide. Go down behind the houses. Don't fire until they all get in the square."

"What's their uniform like, Cap'n?" Tom Davidson asked plaintively. "I've never seen a Spaniard."

"Uniform? Blast if I know. Do you Etty?"

"They got a mess of different ones. As I recollect, though, some have white pants and green coats."

"That's enough to know. Just don't fire on any soldier in brown and black or red and white, and we'll be all right."

Mark followed Simon and his column behind the row of miserable huts. There were no fences or gardens to impede their way. As they passed the huts the column melted into the shadows of the fading light. Behind the last hut Mark and Simon paused to load their rifles. Now they could hear a steady tramp, somewhat irregular but growing louder. Far down the road was a moving mass of white and dark. Of Nat and his men there was no sign. Looking back, Mark could just see that the church doors were being pushed closed by four soldiers. Dusk had settled over the land and a half moon was rising.

A shadow slid beside Simon. "We were too late," said Nat hoarsely. "They'd been to Serafina's already. They killed her and fired her hut."

"No!" Simon spoke aloud in his shocked surprise. "Did you shoot any of them?"

"Didn't want to put 'em on guard. They fired those

shots at a woman running away. I'm going to pass the word." The shadow vanished. Peralta waited, empty in the darkness.

Sauntering easily, the soldiers approached the town. Two officers, following the first line, were laughing. At the entrance of the plaza they all halted, the first line raised their rifles and fired down the street. The second line passed through them. As they came abreast Mark raised his rifle. Simon kicked him sharply. The head of the column reached the spreading tree. One of the soldiers looked up, shouted "*Niños*" and fired into the foliage.

From both sides of the square a ragged fire poured into the Spanish troops. Mark fired blindly into the moving rows of men. Some of them dropped, a few set up a shrill screaming. An officer shouted. The rear ranks separated and ran toward the backs of the two lines of huts. Those in the plaza closed up to form a square around the tree and began to fire sporadically.

"Nothing so dangerous as a man who closes his eyes when he squeezes the trigger," remarked Simon as they reloaded.

"This time I'll look," Mark promised, and stepped from behind the hut for a better aim. The gun was at his shoulder when Simon lurched against him and knocked him sideways as a bayonet stabbed towards them. Mark twisted sideways. The gun slipped from his hands; he caught the barrel and brought the butt against the soldier's head. As the man dropped Mark stumbled. A shot went past his shoulder. A Spanish soldier fell behind him.

From the square came shouts of *Inglesias*. Shots and shouts mingled. Two reed huts roared into flames, sending a quick bright light over the plaza and deepening the shadows. Two of the Spanish soldiers sprawled on the ground. A third burst from around the hut. Simon swung his musket and clubbed him on the head.

"Get back in the shadow," he ordered, and dragged Mark after him.

The Spanish were retreating, streaming from between the huts towards the plaza where already the ranks had broken as the soldiers backed rapidly to the road. A group trotted quickly by them. Nat Bowen sprang from the darkness and clubbed the nearest. "That's for Serafina," he shouted. The group turned, bayonets at ready. Simon and Mark dashed forward. Nat was using his musket as a sword to parry a bayonet. Simon swung his musket and stumbled. A bayonet was poised. Mark reached forward to knock it aside. A shout echoed from the road. The soldiers hesitated for a moment and Nat knocked down another. The remainder turned and ran into the blackness. Nat started to follow, but Simon caught his arm.

"Let them go. Let them go," came the calls down the square.

In the wan flames of the dying fires the ground was seen strewn with white clad figures, some still, some moving or groaning. From the branches of the tree dropped six small boys, one with a bleeding shoulder.

"Come in, boys," shouted Olcott.

The men began to converge towards the church. A few were limping, some had blood on their faces, and one man held a broken right arm with his left hand, but when they lined up no one was missing. They looked calm, but faintly pleased.

The church door creaked behind them. The priest squeezed his way through and advanced on the Captain.

Olcott held up his hands at the flood of words. "Etty, what's he saying?" he asked helplessly.

"He's thanking us, sir. I think he says we saved the women and children," allowed Simon doubtfully. "He's saying the soldiers may come back."

"Tell him if they come back to send us a runner. But I don't think they will. They know we'd really wipe them out. Tell him to have the ones there in the square carried as far down the road as possible, all of them. Tell him we're sorry about Serafina and the others. Tell him we don't fight women and children and won't let anyone else."

Simon rubbed the back of his head. "That's more than my Spanish'll stand, sir, but I'll try. Hey, Angelo," he called. "You tell the padre here what the Captain said."

Angelo's shrill voice apparently said all that was needed.

He was just finishing when a boy raced around the corner of the church. "*Hombres de Montañas*" he shouted. "*Nuestros hombres de montañas aquí!*"

Mark glanced toward the shadows, deeper now as the last flares from the burning huts died away, but he could see only a mass that might be a group of men.

Angelo bowed to the priest and to Olcott and ducked around the corner.

The Captain gave a half salute towards the black figure and raised his voice. "All right. Back to camp. Company right."

As the Provincials filed past the church steps the priest raised his hand in blessing. And then they were going at as quick a trot as the half moon and darkness permitted down the narrow road toward the coast.

Olcott mopped his forehead as they came into camp and

the sentries reported no one had been near the place. "Wouldn't have been at all surprised to find Old Put here wanting to know where we'd been without him," he admitted solemnly. "Turn in, men. And we'd better keep this to ourselves."

But when Mark and Simon crawled into their hut they found the place had been turned upside down, beds torn apart, knapsacks emptied. As Mark dropped to sleep on the awkwardly rearranged branches the face of Captain Lamson floated before him.

11

The Results of Carelessness

THANKS to the water from Mama Hanno's spring, most of Captain Olcott's company escaped the fevers and agues that kept one half the English and Provincial troops continually in the hospitals on land or on the rolling ships at sea. Everyone knew bad water and night dampness were dangerous, but nothing could be done about them. But the morning after the expedition to Peralta Simon woke with his eyes unnaturally bright and a flush on his long face.

"It's the old fever, Mark," he said in a queerly fast voice. "Want to tell you quick. It comes with these lands, and once you've had it you'll get it again if you come back. Thought I'd fooled it this time. Don't let them take me to any hospital. That'd be the mortal end of me. Get me drinking water when I'm hot and loan me a blanket when I'm shivering like an aspen leaf, and I'll come out of it in three-four days. And don't mind anything I say, for I won't mean it." He closed his eyes as if he were tired. Mark felt Simon's forehead, and his skin was so hot and dry he jumped.

Angelo crept into the little hut and looked at Simon. "*El Señor* should go to Mama Hanno," he whispered. "She cure him."

Mark looked at him gratefully. "You're right. I'll see the Captain."

Captain Olcott, looking more like a school teacher than ever in his shirt sleeves, with iron-rimmed glasses on his beaked nose, listened impassively to Mark's plea. "Sorry about Etty," he said. "Too good a man to turn over to those medicos. It's not regular to let him be cured by that old witch, but then nothing's regular in this army here. If you and Davidson can't get him there alone take some of the men. Make him understand he's to stay until he's well. I've seen these agues. They can pass in a few days, or take a man off in an hour. All right. What you waiting for? Go take him there."

At first Simon didn't understand what they were doing and tried to fight them both, then collapsed into a mumbling that was incoherent and frightening. At last he could walk with an arm on the boys' shoulders, but it took an hour to get him to the hut above the spring. Angelo and Mama Hanno were waiting. Angelo with an axe and hatchet.

"Mama Hanno say build hut for *El Señor* there," he pointed to an open spot beneath a mango tree. "Just branches. She say she cure."

It took all morning to make the hut and thatch it with palm fronds Angelo brought from somewhere and then make a bed of cedar and corn stalks.

"Wish we had some honest balsam for this bed," Tom said as he tried to stick the small cedar twigs into the network of larger branches. "Nothing like a good balsam bed, with a good fire in front of you, and the stars so bright they look like they'd been shined." His voice was wistful. "I'd give a pretty to be lying on one now myself."

Mark caught his breath. He could almost smell the sweet pungency of the balsam, hear the crackle and hiss of the dry pine in the fire, feel the cool night air of the hills. "I'd like to be with you," he muttered, "but we aren't, so we better finish this."

When it was done, and Simon stretched on one blanket with Mark's blanket beside him, Mama Hanno waved them away. "She say you leave alone," Angelo translated. "She say *El Señor* back three-four days."

Mark was on wood-gathering detail that afternoon. As Nat pointed out, it was lucky they didn't have much to eat because if they had they would need more wood and that would mean real hard work. As it was, with the English using the good wood of the Cavannas hill for themselves, the puny wood from this puny forest matched the puny meals. Mark laughed and moved away. It was the first chance he had had to be by himself and think about his search. Well, since everything had been moved from the Casa Hermosa to the Casa Alta, he would have to go to Casa Alta. He'd have to find out where it was. And he couldn't go soon enough. He and Simon had agreed on that. But how? He hacked morosely at a dead cedar. He wasn't very bright if he couldn't think of something. Well, he'd start by asking Angelo.

Over the stew at mess that evening, sitting apart at the edge of the firelight, he asked about Casa Alta. Angelo's small dark head bobbed vigorously. Yes, it was up in the hills where the air was cooler. For summer it was used. It was not hard to find. One walked and one asked. How far? Angelo shrugged. He had never been there, but a day's walk, or a night's, perhaps.

If a night's walk should do it that would mean he could be back by the next night. "What road does one take?"

"At the Casa Hermosa one turns right. The road is straight toward the hills. One crosses one, two, three roads. At the fourth one turns left toward the hills. After that one asks."

It sounded simple, too simple, but he had to do it. "Angelo, can you bring me some clothes to wear? I'm going to Casa Alta now."

Angelo flashed him a quick look, then nodded. "I bring."

While he waited in the hut Mark debated as to whether he should tell Olcott what he was doing. But he was reluctant to explain the whole story again, and nothing short of the whole tale would satisfy the skeptical Captain. The best thing would be just to vanish. There was a chance he might not be caught, for drill and roll call were infrequent. He'd tell Tom he was going off and to cover up for him, and trust to luck.

Tom's broad freckled face looked worried at the thought of Mark going alone on some wild errand. "You can't talk the lingo," he protested. "And I don't know what's on your mind, but it doesn't make sense to me. What'll you do if you're caught? And you can't walk far in that outfit and not get caught." He pointed to the brown trousers and gaiters.

"I'm not wearing this," Mark said. "And the country's

filled with people running away from the English, or running to Havana, or just running around. I don't think I'll be noticed. And I won't be gone long."

"What'll I do if you don't come back?"

"Wait three days. Simon should be almost well by then. He'll know where I went and think of something. Stall off the Captain, and if Edward Manning comes over just say I'm off somewhere."

"I don't like it," Tom said flatly. "And I don't think you're right bright. But I'll do it for you." His handshake was solemn as though it might be the last.

Back at the hut Angelo was waiting, clutching a white bundle. "Is better change in woods," he whispered. Mark nodded and looked around. He couldn't take his musket, of course, or anything but his hatchet. He tidied the hut, placed his tricorne and canteen on top of his knapsack, and eased out the back wall after the small figure.

About a mile from camp, not far from the road, a mahogany tree spread its branches above a little hummock. Here, in the light from the rising moon, Mark changed into the short white trousers and white shirt that all the country men seemed to wear. They fitted quite well.

"Was padre's," whispered Angelo. "Roberto's too small. Now I tie these things there." He stood on Mark's shoulders and caught the lowest branch where he tied, with a length of vine, the bundle made of the uniform. "Is safe there and easy to find," he explained. "Now I walk with you. Then tomorrow night I wait here. Wait each day, night."

"I hope I won't be long," Mark laughed uneasily. "If I'm not back the third day tell *El Señor* Simon all this."

At the road that led to Casa Hermosa they parted. "Is straight," Angelo repeated. "If you hear mens, go in forest.

Now many *paisanos,* who must fight at Habana, are being taken by the army. Are also *bandidos,* how you say, outlaws, who have run away from casas. Have care at third road. That to Guanamacoa where peoples, *soldados. Adios, Señor.*" They shook hands formally.

The white road ran straight south. In spite of the daily thunderstorms the dirt was powdery and soft, but Mark was glad he had kept his boots. He knew he could never have marched thirty miles or more on bare feet, in spite of Angelo's assurance that bare feet were best for walking. He passed the Casa, ghostly in the moonlight, and mounted a small hill between open fields. There followed fields of corn and a tall slender cane he did not know, all dotted by palm trees that looked like feathers on top of a stick. Once a dog barked in the distance, and once an owl hooted. The moon, more than half full, crossed the sky as he marched steadily, alone in a black and white land. The third crossroads he skirted cautiously. Now there was an open forest of tall trees on either side of the road.

He was sure he had come twenty miles at least and wondering when he could get some sleep, when he walked into trouble. The land had been rising steadily. He thought he could see the fourth road ahead through the tree trunks and decided he would sleep in another hour. He had felt alone and secure for so long he had ceased even to glance into the woods. Yes, he was approaching the crossroads. Here he would turn left. He sighed with relief.

Two men sprang at him from the roadside and seized his arms. They were short and stocky and strong. One gabbled something at him. Furious at his carelessness, Mark stood still. Perhaps if they let go his arms he could run for it. He looked at one man and said *"Por favor."* A "please" should suit any emergency. One said something and when Mark did not answer jerked him angrily. The two talked a moment, then, still holding his arms, marched him toward the crossroad, turned left, and then into a wide path. Ahead Mark could see, in a shallow valley, the dull glow of a campfire and white clad figures asleep around it. The two men kicked one awake. He nodded, trotted away, and returned with an officer who was hastily buckling on his sword.

The officer was young, and from the way he brushed anxiously at his white uniform probably a new one. When he faced Mark he placed his hand consciously on the hilt of the sheathed sword and the other on the pistol in his wide black belt. In the firelight Mark could see that he had a long sallow face and large eyes with a crease between them that made him look worried.

Both Mark's captors spoke at once. The officer nodded and looked at Mark with concern. Mark said *"Por favor"* again, and wished he had listened to Angelo and Simon. The young man looked more worried than ever. The man who had been kicked awake pointed to Mark and ran a finger across his own throat. The officer shook his head. It was as well he could not make himself understood, Mark thought despondently, for he would surely have said the wrong things. At last, after more talk, a rope was found and Mark was lead to a sapling where he was allowed to lie down before his hands were tied behind his back and the rope then tied to the tree. For good measure, his feet were tied. He looked at the red coals of the fire and prepared to wait for what dawn would bring.

He woke only when his feet were being untied. Now he could see that the camp was under the branches of a tre-

mendous wide-spreading ceiba. His hands were freed, the
rope wound around his waist, and, a captor on either side,
he was led to the circle around the fire. Some fifty
swarthy little men were sitting cross-legged eating something that looked like potatoes that were being pulled from
the ashes. One was tossed to Mark. It was so hot and his
hands so numb he dropped it, which made the men laugh.
When he could break it open it was orange inside and
smooth and sweet. The second was as good as the first. It
was followed by a long yellow fruit with a thick skin and
pale slippery flesh. He was half way through when he was
jerked to his feet.

The officer, looking more worried than ever, was talking
to him. When Mark only shook his head the young man
threw up his hands in despair and gestured to the two men
and pointed westward. They rolled their eyes at each other.

"You seem to be in trouble, young sir," murmured a soft
voice behind Mark. A plump little man with skin of a pale
tan, in blue and white striped shirt and trousers, was standing at his shoulder. "Perhaps you would permit me to be of
service?" The English was formal, but the voice had a
strange upward lilt and accent that was not like the English
he had heard among the troops. The tawny eyes were in-
scrutable.

"I'd be glad of your help," Mark told him quickly.
"What are they saying?"

"The lieutenant, his name is di Balbieno, is saying he does
not know what to do with you. He thinks he had better
send you to Havana where you will be shot as a spy. The
two men wish to cut your throat and take your boots." It
was all said matter-of-factly in smooth, sweet tones.

The officer asked something abruptly. "He wants to

know who you are and where you came from and what you are doing," the soft voice continued.

"Tell him I come from *America del Norte*," said Mark, "and that I was tired of the camp and wanted to see something of the country."

"You cannot think of a better story than that, young sir? No? I will then try to make it convincing." The Spanish that followed was eloquent, but the lieutenant answered forlornly, shrugged his shoulders, shook his head and walked away toward the wide trunk of the tree where a cape was spread over some upright stakes to make a shelter. The two men exclaimed together and sat down, jerking Mark to earth.

"He did not believe you. He is sure you are a spy to find out the strength of the army that is being assembled in the hills to aid the city in the siege. He says he is a kind man and does not like to kill you but you will die anyway, whether he sends you to Havana or keeps you here."

None of this seemed real to Mark. The rising sun was flooding beneath the branches. Pale smoke rose from the ashes. The men had either returned to sleep or were sharpening axes or old-fashioned pikes. They certainly did not look like soldiers. Only one stack of muskets, perhaps ten in all, was in sight.

"You may not believe, young sir, but what he says is true," the voice behind him continued. "I would not care to be in your boots, for I would not feel I would be in them long."

"Who are you?" Mark asked, starting to turn.

"Do not look around, young sir. They might prevent our talking. I am Georgie Smith, of Jamaica, at your service."

"How'd you ever get here?"

"By boat and the kindness of Lord Albemarle. He sent to our Governor for five hundred slaves to help make sandbags for the redoubts of his army. Too many of his own soldiers were sick, as you must know. And so we came, perhaps two weeks ago, and made sandbags and it was very wearying labor, for the dirt is too hard to dig and I do not like to sew. Also the food was atrocious and I was wasting away. Since the guards were careless I decided I might fare better in the interior of the island among my own people. But now I am not at all sure. The food has been scanty and uncertain."

"I'm glad you're here anyway," Mark told him. "Perhaps you can persuade the lieutenant not to send me to Havana."

"Have no hope of that, young sir. He will go and think about what is his duty and then do it. This is his first command, and it is very important to him. Besides, I am now a soldier of Spain."

"These aren't soldiers!"

"They are almost soldiers. The Spanish in Havana are sending in to the country for the slaves and the peasants to be gathered into bands to fight, or to defend the city when it is stormed. There are few arms, most would have only pikes or axes or knives, but the Spanish believe their numbers would be helpful in overwhelming the English."

Mark twisted sideways. Georgie Smith had a round face the color of strong tea with milk in it, a round pursed little mouth, round eyes of pale brown, and a bland smile. It was impossible to guess his age.

"Help me escape," Mark urged. "I . . . I'll get you back safely to camp," he added recklessly.

"But I have no desire to return to camp and fill sandbags," Georgie Smith pointed out peacefully. "What could you pay me to help?"

Mark thought of his few shillings, of the little farm, and shook his head. "I can't pay you a thing," he said sullenly, and turned back toward the circle.

The officer approached again, looked more worried than ever, and gestured with both hands to the two men. He waved to the west and poured out a torrent of words. The men said something. The officer nodded and walked away.

"They said they couldn't walk on an empty stomach, and quite right too," Georgie Smith said cheerfully. "They're going to wait for a meal. The hunters are due back any minute now. Then they will take you to the general in Havana, if they bother to go that far."

12

Escape — and El Gallo

THE hunters did indeed return soon with two wild pigs slung on poles. The pigs were thrust deep in the ashes and the fires replenished above them.

"That should take at least three hours to cook properly," Georgie observed thoughtfully. "But I do not trust them to cook properly. It is too bad. Roast pig can be very good. I am always careful of my food."

Mark wormed his way backward until he could lean against a tree. He was curious about this Georgie Smith. "How does it happen that you speak English so well?" he asked.

This time the plump smile was superior. "But Jamaica is a colony of England, just as is your own colony, whatever that may be. English is our language. The most intelligent of the house slaves are always taught good English, and of course belong to the Church of England. Spanish I speak because my mother had belonged to a Spanish family. Also I know a little French because of a grandmother. If my other grandmother had lived long enough I would have learned Arabic. And I am extremely clever at figures."

In spite of himself Mark was impressed. "If you know all that why are you a slave?" he asked hesitantly.

Georgie was not at all embarrassed. "Because my parents and my grandparents were also slaves. But I am a very trusted bookkeeper for Mr. William Grandison of Spanish Town, as was my father before me."

"Then why were you sent here to Cuba?"

A cloud passed over the smooth cherubic face. "It could be a long and sad story, young sir. But, to put it briefly, I was caught, so to speak, with my hand in the till."

The picture was too much for Mark and he burst into laughter. One guard opened his eyes sleepily and closed them. The smell of roasting pork hovered faintly in the still air. Georgie looked at him reproachfully. "But it is not for laughing. Mr. Grandison lost his best clerk, and I, I discovered sandbags."

"What happened?" Mark tried to stop laughing.

"To me it was all clear and laudable. A slave, you understand, may purchase his freedom, if a price is mutually agreed upon. In a light-hearted moment, after a delicious dinner at the governor's palace, Mr. Grandison agreed to fifty pounds as my price. So, since I had charge of the purchase of supplies, the payment of bills, the shipping of the sugar cane from the estate, I began to gather my pennies and shillings. 'Take care of the pennies and the pounds will take care of themselves,' as the old saying is, young sir. Finally I had thirty pounds. But I grew impatient. Never grow impatient, young sir. I—er—annexed two pounds instead of the usual ten shillings on a shipment of cloth for the field hands. It was too obvious. Mr. Grandison can be clever when he wishes. He did me the honor of beating me himself and then sent me to the governor to be shipped to help Lord Albemarle. And he promised when I was returned from Cuba I would go into the cane fields." The pale brown eyes dimmed with self-pity. "It is a question which is worse, sandbags or sugar cane," he added simply. "That is my problem."

Mark choked. "Yes, it is a problem," he agreed gravely.

"And now," the gentle voice went on, "I suggest we sleep or these so-called soldiers might become annoyed at us both. I do not like it when people are annoyed."

Although he was not used to sleeping at odd moments, Mark found it quite easy to drift off while in the process of thinking about his own problem of escape.

A delicious smell of roasting pork woke him. The pigs had been pulled from the fire and were being carved by anything at hand. Georgie brought Mark some of the meat on a piece of bark and another yam and a portion of a sweet juicy fruit he said was called pineapple.

"I do this as a kindness," he pointed out, as he sat down beside Mark. "Those others would not care if you starved, since they are sure you are not long for this world anyway."

The men around the fire ate greedily. The lieutenant sat by himself at his shelter. Then everyone went to sleep. Mark waited for the snores around him to be unanimous and then started to pick at the rope that circled his waist. He did not dare use his hatchet, which was still hidden by the long white shirt, so all he had for a tool was a sharp edge of a stone. He succeeded in fraying the rope a little and glanced around. Across the circle a sentry was watching him. Mark went to sleep again.

The sun was halfway down the sky when suddenly the camp awoke briskly. The lieutenant assumed a martial air and sent squads of men into the woods with curt orders. Then he strode towards Mark, gestured firmly to the west, and obviously ordered the men on the way. They gave a half-salute, and set off through the woods on a narrow path, with Mark between them, the rope held by the man in front. As he left he heard Georgie call "Good-by, young master." Mark did not answer.

The path was quite clear as it wound around spreading ceibas, beneath towering mahoganies, or plunged into oak thickets. From many of the trees hung curious vines that twined and twisted on themselves like snakes and even hung down from branches to dangle in the path. After ten minutes the man in the rear called something but the one in front shook his head. Mark realized he had better act quickly. He began to remember tales of escaping from the Indians, but nothing seemed to fit his case. He knew both men were thickset and obviously used to hard work. He could not tackle both at once. And there was the rope still about his waist, in a double knot with both ends in the hand of the man in front.

A vine brushed his face. He looked up at it and stopped. The man behind bumped into him while the one in front halted and looked back inquiringly. Mark gestured at the vine, reached up, and began to pull at it. He found it was not one vine but several twisted together. Mark gestured and the man shrugged, then gave a cackle of a laugh as he called out a word, and pulled out a long knife that had been honed down from a bayonet and cut the vine above Mark's head. As he trotted forward again Mark began to wind the vine into a hank. In spite of the small leaves it slipped easily. At one end he made a noose and slip knot, and all the time trotted closer to the man in front.

As the path twisted around a thicket Mark darted ahead, dropped the noose over the arms of the front man, pulled it tight and punched the man on the jaw. The man staggered and dropped. Mark whirled to face the second man, ducked the upswung knife and punched him twice in the stomach. The man dropped the knife and doubled up. Seizing the knife Mark hacked at the rope, slipped it into a noose and dropped it around the shoulders of the man before he could straighten, and whipped the other piece around the threshing feet. The second man was up, trying to tear at the tough vine. Mark punched him again on the jaw and then in the stomach. More vines tied the feet and the two pairs of hands. He made sure the knots were secure, stuffed some leaves in the furiously working mouths and rolled the men off the path into a thicket.

He sat down and wiped his forehead. He was free, but Casa Alta was further away than ever.

"Very nice, young sir," said the approving voice of Georgie Smith as he stepped from behind an oak tree. "Other nations should learn to use their fists as do the English."

Mark gaped at him. "Do you mean to say you were there all the time and never came to help me?"

"But, as I told you, I am now a soldier of Spain," Georgie pointed out reprovingly. "I could not fight my own side. It was quite enough that I did not assist it."

He moved forward into the path. Mark saw the pale eyes dart to the knife by the path. He rose and put his foot on it just as the plump figure started to bend. "That's my knife, Georgie," he pointed out softly. "I won it by my fists." He found the sheath that had held it and strapped it to his own belt.

Georgie watched him sorrowfully. "You do not trust me, young sir?"

"No," Mark told him cheerfully. "And let's cut out this young sir and master. You can call me 'Mr. Mark.'" He had heard the squire's children addressed that way and suddenly it seemed to him proper. "And now you can go back to camp and tell them."

"Oh, no." Georgie sat down. "I think I will join you in wherever you are going. It might be interesting. The food could not be worse."

"But you just joined the Spanish," Mark pointed out, laughing.

"A man must look out for himself. And to me you are more sympathetic, and intriguing. Furthermore, I did not truly wish to join the Spanish. I just joined to eat. Now I will go with you. I have a feeling that if I do I will ultimately eat well."

Surely Georgie's glib Spanish could not help but be useful. "All right," Mark agreed. "But you'll have to earn your way. Do you know how to get us around the camp to the eastward? And you probably won't get anything to eat tonight."

"I thought of that, so I ate as largely as possible," Georgie told him smugly. "And I do know the paths for I was here several days—er—reconnoitering—before the new army descended upon me. Come, Mr. Mark."

"I'm coming. But remember this knife is loose in the sheath and made for throwing. At the first sign of treachery . . ."

"I do not betray my own side," said Georgie with dignity. "Follow me."

He did indeed know the paths that circled the camp of

the recruits and then led towards the east, for they swung south in a wide circle and then towards the hills.

"Soon, now, we will have to ask our way," Georgie said an hour later. "Where did you say you were going, Mr. Mark?"

"You know perfectly well I never said," Mark answered shortly.

"Of course. But if we are to find the way I must ask." The tone was patiently reasonable. "And since you do not speak Spanish nor look Spanish I suggest that you keep your head down and say nothing, except perhaps a faint '*por favor*,' while I do the talking. I will say you are my idiot brother."

In spite of himself Mark had to laugh. "They won't believe that. Better not commit yourself. I want to find the Casa Alta. It belongs to the Peneranda family."

"Indeed? Well, it will be helpful to know that much."

The land was open again, now, the forests left behind, and ahead rose some low gray hills with the dark line of trees on top. The path ran between fields of the tall slender stalks. Georgie stopped and pointed. "Cut two of those, Mr. Mark, and we will more enjoy our journey."

He took one and began to chew the end. Cautiously Mark imitated him and found he was chewing something sweet and stringy and pulpy at the same time. "Sugar cane," explained Georgie. "My future enemy, but now my friend."

It was another half hour, and the sun was low, when they traced a faint smudge of smoke to its hut. As Georgie had suggested, Mark hung his head while the Spanish words rolled around him, and promised himself that he would learn the language before he ever went to a foreign land again.

Finally the peasant allowed them to borrow a gourd and drink from a nearby brook and gave them each a baked yam. As they left the man pointed to the hills and then to the sky. Georgie nodded. As they returned to the path he stepped aside and pulled two dark objects from a tree.

"These are mangoes," he explained, "and ripe. That man could have given us more to eat, if he wished." The mango proved to be yellow and smooth and quite the best fruit Mark had ever tasted. "They are good for the health, if one does not eat too many," Georgie informed him as he carefully wiped his mouth with his shirt.

"But what did he say about Casa Alta?" Mark demanded.

"It is not far. It is up on the top of those hills. We can follow this path, or the road we will soon see to the left. He does not know if anyone is at the Casa." He glanced sideways at Mark.

"What was that last bit he added?"

"He says a storm will descend on us soon. That there are many caves in the hillside in which to shelter if we can reach them in time. We can wait there, and when it is over go on to the Casa."

Mark glanced behind him. The familiar piles of white clouds were creeping along the western sky. It would be good to be out of the rain for once. "All right. Let's make for the caves."

"There are many caves in Cuba," observed Georgie, as they began to trot. "This I have heard. It is because the hills and mountains are made of a strange rock that encourages caves. Sometimes there are also underground rivers. Jamaica has caves also," he added quickly.

It became a race between the advancing clouds, the growing dusk and their tired legs. From the fields of sugar cane, dotted with low palms, they entered a land of corn and then a sparse wood of cedars and small oaks. The cliffs were before them as the first thunder rolled gently. They began to scramble up the hillside on a path sunken between low banks as though hundreds of feet had worn it down over hundreds of years. Georgie hurried along, reached a ledge, paused, shook his head, and followed the path along the side of the hill. Behind a thick grove they found a cave entrance just as the first drops of rain splattered on the leaves. A lightning flash showed this was no little cave such as Mark had found occasionally in the hills of Connecticut. This was a cavern, stretching into unknown depths of blackness, higher than two men could reach. The floor was thick with a soft gray dust. Rude benches had been hacked out along the walls of the entrance. Here, quite safe from the downpour, they sat and shivered in the quick coolness.

As he watched the sheets of water, lit to a silvery brightness by the lightning, Mark realized that this was the night Angelo would begin to wait for him. He must get back, and before Captain Olcott missed him, and before Simon was well enough to worry. He thought of the long miles between him and the coast. How far was Casa Alta anyway, and what would he find there, beside the portrait? Beside him Georgie had been talking softly of Jamaica. Mark dropped his hand on the knife and let his head fall forward. He would nap while he could.

A sharp kick on his leg aroused him. "Ghosts!" Georgie was babbling beside him. "Wake, Mr. Mark. Ghosts!"

Mark shivered at the word as much as at the steaming dampness. The rain had stopped and the clouds had passed. A pale yellow sky in the west threw a pallid light into the cave. Cautiously he looked to the right.

In the dimness he could discern a motionless row of white figures. They had no legs below the short white trousers. If there were heads he could not see them. And they did not move. Georgie was crowding against him, his hands with the first two fingers crossed, held before his face. "I cannot be brave with ghosts," he moaned.

Mark gulped and shook his head. His father had always said there were no ghosts. But there were the figures. He could feel the hair rise at the back of his neck.

Georgie sprang to his feet. "If they have no legs they cannot follow us," he whimpered, tugging at Mark's arm. "Run."

Mark rose in spite of himself and turned toward the entrance. It was filled with men who had drifted, as silently as falling leaves, to fill the whole opening. But at least they were men, for one was marching toward them.

Mark glanced back into the cave. The white figures were moving forward. He almost laughed. They were men too, who had been standing behind one of the low stone benches so their legs had been hidden, and their heads had been behind a low overhanging of rock. He was ashamed he had been so frightened.

Georgie laughed weakly. "I was hasty in my assumption," he admitted shakily.

To Mark's eyes, the men in the cave looked exactly like the recruits of Lieutenant di Balbieno, except that their clothes were somewhat more ragged and he could see no muskets. The leader was distinguished by a black hat, a high curving affair that could be worn either lengthwise or crossways on the head and looked vaguely both nautical or military. Some leaves with which it had been stuffed

134

hung on either side of the alert brown face. He also wore a leather belt and a large double-barreled pistol. As he listened to the exchange in Spanish between this man and Georgie, Mark wished again he had tried to learn a few words at least from Angelo. In the middle of a sentence the leader's eyes lighted on the knife at Mark's belt. At a gesture another man ran forward and tried to seize it. Regretfully Mark slid the sheath off his belt and thereby also lost his hatchet. The leader appropriated them both with a pleased smile. Georgie watched with a bright smile.

A few more words, and the men were swarming towards the back of the cave, Mark and Georgie in the midst. "We are going to eat," Georgie told him happily. "Then they will decide what to do with us. They are a band of outlaws, though they would not care for the word. The leader calls himself El Gallo, which means cock."

"At least they won't send us to Havana," grunted Mark, stumbling in the gloom.

"That might have been preferable," Georgie answered seriously.

The entrance cave narrowed to a passage that turned and entered into a large cavern that could have held five hundred men. The smoke from two fires moved steadily towards the blackness beyond, showing there must be still another cave or vent. Georgie nodded approvingly. "This is more comfortable than the open air and the hard ground."

Some women moved about two iron kettles, and soon a stew of meat and vegetables in bark bowls was brought to them. Georgie smacked his lips. "This is better eating than the army."

El Gallo moved over to talk to Georgie. Mark peered

through the light and shadows. He could see some old-fashioned pikes leaning against one wall and a pile of axes, but no other arms.

"These people have no concern with the English," Georgie told him, after a few minutes, "except that they hope the English will take the island from the Spanish. El Gallo says they have all run away from bad masters, which, alas, I can understand. Their chief problem is that they have no arms with which to fight. Also that makes it difficult sometimes to take the food they need, since there are not even enough knives to go around."

"But what about us?" asked Mark irritably.

"He is thinking about us. He has asked if we would care to join his band, since we both look quite strong."

"Don't say yes or no," Mark ordered. "We can think ourselves."

"As you wish. But I venture to suggest that since these men are not sympathetic to slave owners we do not ask about the place you seek."

Mark nodded absently. He was seeing the stack of muskets under the ceiba tree. "Tell him we know where he can get some guns and other weapons if he wishes. But he must take us with him."

Georgie looked aghast. "That will mean walking those miles again."

"But then they will be glad to have us join," Mark told him. "And, by that time . . ." his voice trailed away.

El Gallo grinned broadly when he heard about the arms of the recruits. "*Pues* . . ." he exploded. "*Pronto,*" and began to shout.

Once more in the center of the column, Mark and Georgie marched from the cave to the open hillside, to the

north and a road at right angles, and to the west. Georgie
had been whispering to the man beside him. Now he gestured to the east where a faint glow was spreading behind
the line of black trees.

"This road goes to the place," he told Mark, "up the hill
and beyond the crest. A few miles only. But I see no chance
for us to be free to find it."

Mark was wondering if his idea was so good after all, if
they had to walk all the way back to the camp of the recruits, and did not answer. But only some three miles had
been covered when a figure came racing up the road to
gabble excitedly to El Gallo. Georgie pushed forward,
pointing out it was best to be as near headquarters, or in
this case, as near to a head hat, as possible. When the excited
sounds had died away El Gallo gave some orders and pushed
Mark and Georgie into the bushes beside the road. The sky
above was blue and luminous. The road stretched emptily to
left and right.

"The lieutenant and his army are marching this way,"
whispered Georgie, as he shifted away from a root. "It is
not known if they seek us, the outlaws, food, or recruits."
El Gallo thwacked him on the head and Georgie crouched
lower.

It was five minutes before the recruits were heard, an
irregular, casual sound of many feet, none in step. They
came down the road, four abreast, slouching and talking.
Lieutenant di Balbieno marched stiffly in front, his sword
held upright.

Mark poked Georgie. "Tell El Gallo not to kill anyone."

Georgie whispered, turned and sniffed. "He says it is his
business and not yours. But he adds that he is not a fool.
Why should he kill men who are just the same as his own?

He will see that they all join his band, except for those who fight."

Then the group on the road was surrounded by a leaping shouting mass. El Gallo fired his pistol in the air and sprang to face the young officer. Patting the lieutenant on the shoulder, he snatched the sword and waved it in the air and fired the other barrel of the pistol in triumph. In the road men swayed and fought in unconvincing fashion.

Mark sprang to his feet. "All right. They'll be busy for a while. Come along."

Georgie looked at him in dismay. "You are leaving now? To walk more? But this is madness!"

Mark pulled him to his feet. "Come along. I'm going to Casa Alta, and you're going with me. Remember?"

Georgie looked at him speculatively. "All right. I'll come," he agreed quickly, and plunged into the woods.

By instinct or knowledge he found a path towards the hills and trotted forward with surprising speed. The sounds of gentle combat faded behind them.

"What will happen to the lieutenant?" asked Mark. He had felt sorry for the worried young man.

"Oh, he'll be turned loose after a while and return to Havana and be promoted because of the dangers he encountered in the line of duty. The Spanish do not look on fighting and duty as do the English."

With this, Georgie concentrated on walking.

13

At
Casa Alta

THEY came to the white walls of Casa Alta before moon-set. The iron gates at both the front and back were securely fastened. Mark's first impulse was to climb the wall, but then he realized this would be very stupid.

"There are some huts or stables," said Georgie, pointing towards a group of palms. "We could sleep. My legs will begin to scream of their own accord if I make them walk farther."

Mark laughed and followed him. Sleep was the wisest course. After looking in one or two empty huts they curled up beneath a palm.

By daylight Casa Alta still looked deserted, but then Mark noticed the iron gate was ajar and some hens were high-stepping into the outer world. Mark ran to the gate and thrust his foot in the open space.

"*Buenas dias,*" panted Georgie behind him. "*Por favor . . .*"

With a clucking sound not unlike the hens the gate opened wider on a middle-aged, gray-haired woman in a short blue cotton dress. She stepped back in surprise and Mark and Georgie followed her inside the walls.

"And now," said Georgie, in a smooth silky voice, "you had better tell me what you are here for. Is it plate? Or gold?"

Mark made his face stay immobile. This was no time to show either anger or surprise. "Neither," he answered curtly. "Tell her my uncle was *El Señor* Thad. That he told me to come here and look for Beltran, and to look at the house."

The pleasant face lighted with a smile at the names. "She says she remembers *El Señor* T'ad," Georgie translated, "but that Beltran is not here. For sometime he has been in the hills farther east. She is alone in the house. She will show it to us." His voice grew warmer. "She says she will give us breakfast. Mr. Mark, even though you seek nothing here it is worth coming for an egg."

The well in the flower-filled patio provided Mark his first bath in weeks, and when he sat down in the kitchen to eggs and fresh bread and a dark brown drink Georgie said was cocoa he began to feel that the journey had all been worth-while. Evidently no marauding parties had reached this peaceful spot. How he would carry a heavy portrait over the miles between here and the coast he did not see. But perhaps there would be something to copy and he would not need the whole picture. Birds fluttered in wooden cages, a purple vine festooned one side of the balcony that surrounded the patio, the air was fresh and cooler than the coast. He could understand the charms of Casa Alta.

As she served them, the woman chattered eagerly with Georgie. "This is Maria Theresa," he finally announced.

"The servants and slaves ran away some time ago. But she had no where to go and so stayed. She was the cook. And a good one, too," he added thoughtfully. "She says the soldiers do not come so far from Havana, and the outlaws leave her alone because they know Beltran and his men will guard her."

Mark pushed back his chair. "Good. Now ask her to show us the house, please."

As they entered the high, dark *Salle Grande* Mark's heart sank. Heavy chairs ranged the walls, but these and the table were the only things in the room, no rugs on the tile floor, no tapestries on the paneled wall, no portraits above the fireplace. Hopefully he followed Maria Theresa from room to room. Only a few beds, chairs, chests, tables too heavy to move, remained. One large chest contained nothing but old-fashioned clothing. From the last bedroom they returned to the gay patio. Mark knew his shoulders were sagging.

"Ask her what happened to the furnishings," he ordered harshly.

"If you would tell me," Georgie began, then threw up his hands at Mark's expression and turned to Maria Theresa. "She says that what belonged here and what was brought here from the Casa by the coast were all taken to Havana six weeks and more ago. The wagon loads from Casa Hermosa were not even unpacked. Someone had made a mistake in bringing them here. The *Señor* Peneranda wished everything safe in Havana. He was very angry. He was so angry he shot the man who made the mistake."

"Did *everything* go?" Mark exclaimed.

"All but what you see."

Mark sat down on a bench, his eyes fixed on a bush with

flaming red flowers. "Thank her," he said dully. "And thank her for the breakfast, too." If the curious tawny eyes had not been watching him so intently he knew he would have cried. Once more the portrait of Don Diego had eluded him. Could he go to Havana now? Again common sense spoke. He must get back to the coast and the army. "Ask her if she knows anyone who could guide us back to the Rio Coximar," he directed.

At Georgie's query Maria nodded cheerfully. "She will summon her nephew by a gong," Georgie said, "and he will gladly, for the sake of your *El Señor* Thad, act as guide."

Mark waited on the bench and dozed and watched Georgie and Maria preparing lunch. Georgie was directing, and Maria was smiling and bustling from hearth to table. The meal was wild pigeon, broiled, and strange fruits and vegetables more taste-filled than anything in Connecticut. He wished he could ask what they were so he could tell Debby, but now he was eating alone and in state in the dining room while Maria and Georgie giggled and chattered in the kitchen. As he finished Georgie sidled up beside his chair.

"Was it the plate you were after?" he asked softly. "Maria says there was much, some gold, much silver, but that it went on the wagons."

Mark shook his head. "I don't know anything about gold and silver plate."

"But you were looking for something in each room. Your face showed that." In the silence that followed Georgie shrugged and vanished.

When Mark had washed again and had been introduced

to a lively youth called Cuarto, because he was the fourth son, Maria shyly brought him an earthenware mug.

"It's a *refresco*," said Georgie, "for the road. Fruit juice, pineapple this time."

It was sweet and cool and Mark tried again to thank her for the food and the guide. When Cuarto had swung back the gate Mark followed, and turned to Georgie, who was still standing beside Maria.

"Come along," said Mark gruffly.

Georgie shook his head slowly, a pleased smirk on his smooth face. "Oh no, Mr. Mark. I do not go with you to make sandbags and then be returned to the cane fields of Jamaica. I am staying here, with Maria. She is quite the best cook I know, and good food is so important for one's health."

Mark gaped. "Not go back? What'll you do if the army comes?"

"Which army? Any army I can join. Or I can join the outlaws, who, Maria assures me, have a most pleasant life and normally eat quite well. Or I can stay here. And you and I are quits, for while you rescued me from the Spanish I brought you safely here. And so, good-by and bon voyage, Mr. Mark."

The gate swung shut.

For a moment Mark was angry. Then he began to laugh, and laughing followed Cuarto.

It was a long and difficult march, for Cuarto avoided all houses and villages and scouted the unavoidable roads most carefully before crossing. And there was a short nap in the deepest darkness before moonrise. It was aggravating to Mark to have to rely on pointing and on smiles for communication, but he kept busy as long as possible trying to find out which fruits were good to eat and how to manage the *cana dulce*, or sugar cane. It was when he followed Cuarto in silence that black depression overwhelmed him. Casa Hermosa had seemed so easy that he should have been suspicious of such good fortune. Casa Alta had presented more difficulties, which had turned out to be not at all what he had expected. But now Havana! A city surrounded by walls, filled with the enemy and soon to be besieged by his own people. Of course it would fall, but he was sure that Pedro Peneranda would have sufficient agility and wealth to turn up on the side of the victors, and keep his property intact, and win any court battle Mark might be able to start over the will. He'd never find the Peneranda Hoard now. He stumbled on a root and resolutely concentrated on trying to keep his feet.

He felt badly that he had no present to give Cuarto on parting, but Cuarto obviously expected nothing and cheerfully wished him *Adios* by the Casa Hermosa. Angelo was asleep at the foot of the mahogany tree. After one glance at Mark's face he asked no questions as he helped Mark into the uniform, which seemed more loose than before, and vanished with the white clothes. Gratefully Mark crept into the empty hut.

At mess the next morning Captain Olcott was waiting for him. The steely eyes swept him from head to foot, the thin hand lifted as Mark started to speak. "Don't say anything, Woodbridge," the slightly nasal voice drawled. "Silence is even more golden now. Don't say you were hunting, because you left your musket in the hut. Don't say you were with Simon, for I went to see myself. In short, shut up. If we weren't getting a trifle short of healthy men, because some fools will drink bad water when they go visiting along the lines, I'd confine you to quarters or send you to a ship. So don't try me."

Mark could only gulp, "No, sir."

The Captain moved away and then turned back. "But you may tell me someday in New Haven, if we both get back," he added softly.

So Mark told no one except a white and shaky Simon who returned that afternoon.

14

An Interview
with Captain Lamson

CAPTAIN Olcott kept Mark hard at work the next day at deepening drainage ditches, repairing broken walls of huts, and chopping wood. He had just brought his last load to the cooking fires when a private in the uniform of the New York Provincials came toward him.

"Mark Woodbridge?" he asked. "Cornet Manning sends his regards and asks if you can join him fishing from the shore. He'll wait for you at the mouth of that dry river." The man pointed towards the Coximar and stalked away.

Arranging the wood as the cook demanded Mark began to wonder why Edward would send a Provincial with the message. But of course he might have met the man on the way and decided to spare himself the rest of the hot walk.

Though sometimes the boys had brought some fish to the mess, Mark had not heard of any soldiers trying to fish from the shore. But it was true that just beyond the mouth of the Coximar there were some low cliffs that held the small Spanish redoubt where the water might be deep enough to drop a line. And fish would be welcome. He went in search of Simon, who was not to be found. So he told Tom Davidson about Edward's message, straightened his uniform, and set off for the shore.

When he reached the narrow stony river bed, filled with rough boulders tumbled down by spring freshets from the distant hills, he turned down the right bank. The directions had been very vague. There was no sign of Edward. Perhaps he was in the river bed itself. Mark slid down the steep bank and made his way around the boulders toward the sea.

He was scrambling between surprisingly large rocks when something hard was pushed against his back. "I thought that message would bring you," said the satisfied voice of Lamson behind him. "Just go over and sit by that rock, and we'll have a nice chat."

Mark's first impulse was to turn and try to grapple the man, but the object at his back did feel like a pistol, and it might be loaded. As he stumbled toward the rock, and twisted enough to look back in the process, he saw that Lamson was indeed holding a small pistol. And behind Lamson was the same Provincial soldier, grinning broadly. Mark wanted to knock his head against the rock, for being so stupid as to fall for such an obvious bait. He sat down beside a boulder, his hands on his knees. What did the man propose now?

Lamson sat down in a patch of shade and held his pistol pointed at Mark. "I thought it about time you and I had a talk," he went on, "and it seemed the easy way to separate you from your friend Etty." He raised his voice. "All right, Reed. We'll have our talk. Go back."

The man smiled slyly. "You won't need to raise your voice much, Captain, and I'll be right with you." He backed around a rock.

Lamson kept his pale blue eyes on Mark. "You and I

could be of help to each other," he began, in a now friendly voice. "There's something you want, and I could help you get it, and then you could share it with me."

"I don't know what you're talking about," Mark answered coldly.

Lamson smiled. "If you don't, the man who called himself Pedro Galvez does. He's really Pedro Peneranda, you know, with all the other names tacked on too. One of the nephews of that Don Diego who left Casa Hermosa, and other things, to your uncle. But it isn't just the estate Pedro wants, it's the treasure."

Mark managed to look surprised. "Treasure?"

Lamson nodded, and wet his lips as he repeated the word. "The Peneranda treasure. It was famous. Gold plate, silver plate, jewels from Spain, Peru, from all over. Enough for a king, these days. Gathered for two hundred years."

"I didn't know." It was true; Uncle Thad hadn't written that.

"Question is, where is it? That's what Pedro wants to find out."

"I don't know."

"Perhaps not, now. But you have some way of finding out, or you wouldn't be here. You and that Etty wouldn't go to all this trouble over a house and some lands you couldn't use anyway."

"Uncle Thad said the plate went to the nephews."

"Aaaah, so there was a letter, or some such thing. We weren't sure, just thought it likely a man wouldn't leave that will without some explanation. Pedro wasn't so sure, but I was." His eyes narrowed. "I wonder where it is. It isn't in your tent . . ."

148

Again Mark could have knocked his head on the rock for giving something away so easily.

Lamson leaned forward eagerly. "Listen. You and Etty haven't a chance of getting those jewels, no matter where they are, by yourselves. Oh, I know you went to the Casa with that young sprig from England, and found nothing, and rescued a burro and a boy. Hope you don't meet Gaspar again; he got a beating himself when he reported back to Havana. You can say you went to the Casa out of curiosity, and I won't believe you. You were after something. Pedro is after it, too. He's searched the Casa and the land around and found nothing. But those jewels are somewhere. He's going to get hold of you, and of that letter, and if you won't tell he'll make you, and then cut your throat."

"He'd have a hard time, in the middle of the army," Mark managed.

"He'll do it, when he thinks the time's come. We had several talks in New York. I wouldn't care to be someone in his way. His brother died last year, you know. He told me it was from a wound that got infected, and laughed as though it was a joke.

"But, now, I could take a squad to the Casa, get whatever is there, and bring it back safely and get it on a supply ship going north. We could both get on the ship, and Pedro couldn't put a hand to either of us thereafter."

Mark remembered the implacable black eyes of Mr. Galvez. "He could follow you north and knife you in the back," he suggested.

"He might like to," Lamson admitted, "but he'd know he couldn't find me. With money, jewels, I'd be off to Europe, and Europe's a big place." He wet his lips again.

"With money you can have castles, servants, horses, anything you want. Think of it! The world's yours!"

"How about Shuttleworth? Where does he come in?"

"Bah. I'd give him a diamond, a small one. He'd be satisfied." The pale eyes were alight with eagerness. "And with your share, why the world would be yours, too. But I tell you, without me to help you, and protect you from Pedro, you won't get a thing. What do you say?"

Fascinated by the picture the man had painted, of what untold wealth could bring, Mark had almost forgotten where he was. But the sun blazing on the pale rocks was dazzling. He blinked and shook his head.

"I can't tell you what I don't know."

Lamson's eyes narrowed. "I don't believe you. You may not know enough, but you know something. You're a stupid fool not to take my offer. Come now. Fifty-fifty."

Mark asked something he'd long wondered about. "Why'd this Pedro go and kill Uncle Thad this spring?"

"He knew about the war with England. He was sure if England attacked Cuba she'd take the island and your uncle would turn up then and get everything. Pedro's desperate, I tell you, to get his hands on the jewels before the city falls. Soon as he does he can get away. But between us we can out-fox him, with what you know and I can do."

"I don't know," Mark repeated.

Lamson grimaced, then shrugged. "Then I'll throw in with Pedro. I told him you'd throw in with me—that New Englanders were practical, had good sense, that you'd see reason, and we'd laugh at him together. But I'll have to tell him he was right, and that I'll work with him."

"How're you going to get word to him?" Mark asked interestedly.

"I have my ways." Lamson was lounging against the tall rock, pistol dangling from his hand. His clubbed hair, his uniform, were almost finicky in their neatness. The pale eyes looked at Mark speculatively. "You think I'm a villain," he went on slowly. "I'm not, you know. I just want as much money as I can get, as easily as I can get it, so I can live like a gentleman. Other men get it other ways. But my luck's been bad. Now fate, chance, what you will, brought you and that blasted document to me. And now the Peneranda jewels are the best chance I'll ever have to live the kind of life I should have. I want them, and I'm going to get them. I'd rather do it alone, of course, but," he took a turn in the small space between the boulders, "I know I can't. So I'd rather share with you than with that snake Pedro. You're not a bad lad, you know. I really like you, though that Etty is too nosy. You and I could pull it off together, and I'd play it all fair and square."

"I wouldn't trust you," Mark said in a low voice.

The whole face blazed with rage. "No one questions my word." Then Lamson shrugged and laughed. "Even a gentleman adventurer, as I've been called, can have his pride, you see. I'd like to kill you for that, now." He smiled quite pleasantly, and raised his pistol. "I'd shoot you, but you know the one thing we need." His hand dropped. "On the other hand," he began thoughtfully, "I don't ordinarily like violence, but if I could find out now . . ." He raised his voice. "Reed, come and bring your bayonet."

Mark jumped up and backed against a high boulder. He was hemmed in on all sides and Lamson blocked the only way out. He lowered his head and dove forward, catching Lamson around the waist and pinioning his arms as the pistol went off behind his back. If he could keep behind Lamson when Reed came with the bayonet . . . Their feet were slipping on the pebbles. Lamson was swearing. Footsteps were running.

"Hola, Mark." It was Simon's voice. Relief made Mark loosen his hold. Lamson broke away and swung his pistol at Mark's head, but a hand caught his arm.

"Now, now," said Simon. "Easy does it."

For a second all three stood like statues.

"There's a man running away," drawled Tom Davidson. "Who's he?"

Lamson lowered his arm and Simon let it go. The Captain looked at them. "You've made your choice, Woodbridge. You'll regret it." He put his pistol back in his belt, picked up his hat, turned his back and disappeared up the stream bed.

"What's all that about?" asked Tom, scrambling down a boulder, followed by Nat. "Thought you were going fishing with that English friend, Mark?"

"Captain Lamson interrupted me," Mark managed.

"Well, let's go now. We brought some line and got Smathers to make us some hooks out of some old buckles. I heard some Rhode Islanders got themselves a nice mess the other day," said Tom.

Mark looked at Simon, who just grinned. "Come along. I could do with fish for a change."

So they fished over the parapet of the Spanish redoubt and caught so many of what looked like rock bass the four could scarcely carry them back to camp. There was enough for the company, and Angelo and the boys, and when Mark went for the casks of water the next morning he took two to Mama Hanno. There was no sign of the burro or the young man.

Simon had heard the end of the dialogue with Lamson, so Mark just told him the beginnings during one of the crashing thunderstorms that came so frequently at night and only made the air more hot and humid. At the end he berated himself for going off alone.

"You're wrong," Simon told him strongly, across the thick darkness. "You've got to go on your own. No matter what. It was my thought to come here. And you came along. But young ones mustn't get to thinking they have got to rely on someone older. You've filled out a good piece in these weeks, in spite of the food. You're nigh a man now, and a man's got to learn to rely on himself. And he's got to do what he thinks right, so he can always hold his head high. That's not saying I won't be beside you every chance there is, and if anything goes wrong, I'll be with you. But you mustn't go on thinking first 'What would Simon think or do?' or 'If only Simon were here.' It's what does Mark Woodbridge think and do that matters."

A long rolling crash halted his voice. When the familiar dry tang of the Connecticut hills came again, Mark felt a sudden ache of homesickness for his well-loved father and mother, for Debby, for Uncle Thad, for the comfortable happiness of youth. Perhaps this was growing up, this knowing suddenly that childhood was gone forever and there was no one to direct, or comfort him any more; that there was only himself on whom he could rely.

"You didn't do badly, jumping Lamson that way," the voice in the blackness went on. "And what you gave away he probably knew, mostly, already. We'll have to keep an eye out for Pedro, but it's not likely he'll try to do much until we take the city. Then you can get to the English commander with the will."

"I'm sure glad it's in Old Put's strong box."

"Yup. Safe there. No need to worry. And this isn't much of a war. It won't last much longer."

Later that evening Angelo sidled up to Mark when all the others were out of earshot. "When you want go to Havana you tell me," he whispered.

"Why should I go to Havana?"

"Sssh. Mama Hanno say you have to go. My brother guide you."

"But there's an army, and walls, between me and the city."

Angelo nodded. "*Si*. But Roberto know best way. He boy at Casa with our burro. You help. So he guide you. You tell me." As always, Angelo slipped away.

Mark shivered uneasily.

15

Attack
in the Night

A FISHING expedition that involved nearly a third of the company was organized the next afternoon. Edward arrived just in time to accompany Mark and Tom to the fort on the point where the men lined the stone parapet, leaning out above the bright water to cheer or curse their luck.

At first the others left a discreet space around the three boys. It was Tom who changed everything. "Say, Cornet," he asked suddenly. "How do you like your officers? Yesterday I took a message for Captain Olcott to the English camp, and hung around a bit, watching. Don't know as I'd care for some of them, myself."

"Oh, come now, you know we're not supposed to discuss our own officers," Edward told him cheerfully. "That's practically rebellion."

"You don't say! That takes nigh half the fun out of being in the army."

"What's the other half?" Mark wanted to know. But Tom plowed on.

"We talk 'bout our officers all the time. Can't tell me

you don't too. What do you think of them? We won't peach on you."

The same impish grin Mark had seen that night by the ladder again transformed Edward's rather solemn face. He handed his line to Tom.

"Can't talk if my hands aren't free, you know," he began in a mincing voice. And suddenly he was strutting along the parapet, his chest stuck out, his arms swinging stiffly, his nose in the air, until Mark could see a fat colonel trying to march with dignity. "Rrrrmph," came a surprisingly deep voice. "There's Colonel A. Rrrrrmph. Not the way, er, to, er do things, you know. Not how the King's Own watered its whiskey, my boy. When I was, er, in India, now, things were different, er, very different, my boy."

The soldiers had turned their heads and were watching him silently. Edward seemed oblivious of all except the wide grins of Mark and Tom.

He became a dainty superior officer walking delicately on tiptoe, head cocked on one side, left hand waving a handkerchief, his voice a stylish drawl. "As for Captain B, really, my dear chap, it's quite impossible to have a civilized meal here. And it's no use bringing out good snuff or wine. The wine will be quite spoiled by the rolling of the ship, and the beastly dampness turns the snuff to paste, a most horrid object, I assure you."

Someone stifled a snigger. Tom was gaping, the two fishlines forgotten. Mark marveled as he grinned. Here was still another Edward.

Now he was a martinet drawn stiffly erect. "And for Captain C," he rasped, "that man's queue is one-half inch too long. That man's gaiters have two specks of mud." He was obviously looking down a line of soldiers on parade.

"Those buttons need another polish." His head turned sideways. "And, as you were saying, Captain, the best thing for a colicky horse is champagne mixed with good country ale."

A shout of laughter went up all along the parapet. Edward blinked and was himself again, his face a fiery red. "I didn't mean to do all that," he stammered. "It has just been building up in me for months, and, I haven't had anyone to talk to. I didn't mean to make an ass of myself."

"You didn't," Tom assured him flatly. "You took them off for fair. But if they're like that, how come you can stand them?"

"They aren't all like that." Edward was his composed self again. "Some, like Colonel Carlton or Lieutenant Forbes, are such fine chaps you'd follow them anywhere. And I should tell you that Colonel A was with Clive at Plassey and Captain B lead his men up the heights of Abraham. So you can't tell by an officer's manner what sort of man he is underneath."

Tom shook his head. "How do the men stand them, though?"

"Well, the enlisted men have to. But they like an officer who knows what he's doing, even if he may be odd some ways." He smiled tentatively. "Perhaps I could get a few of our men to come fishing here, if you'd let them. Then you could talk to them yourself."

"You do that," Nat said suddenly. "I've always hankered to know some Britishers and never had a chance. Eh, men? We'll let 'em catch all the fish."

"Sure," echoed several voices. "Send 'em along. We'd like that."

"I'll do what I can," promised Edward, "if you won't give me away. And if I can persuade my captain."

"And thank you for the play-acting," said a rear voice. "Best thing I've seen since New York."

Edward blushed and hurried to take his line back from Tom. The others added fish to his pile until he said he would have to send a squad to fetch them all.

As Mark walked back with him, however, he confided that no officer, not even the lowly rank of Cornet, could be seen carrying anything in his hands. When Mark argued about the awkward situations that would result from such a foolish order they both laughed so hard they had to stop and lean against some rocks.

"What I really came for," Edward got out at last, "was to ask you to a concert this evening which three of the regimental bands are giving."

Captain Olcott raised one eyebrow at Mark's request for permission to join the 9th for the evening, but allowed he could see no harm in a concert, or how even Mark could get into trouble at one.

Mark would have said music could mean nothing to him, but in spite of himself he felt his blood quicken and his foot begin to tap to the stirring rattle of drums, the sweet high shrilling of fifes, and the blare of horns. The concert was held on the parade ground, in a circle of small fires, with the dark trees as background and the light of the rising moon distorting shapes and shadows. The varied uniforms of officers and men made a bright ring of color. One portion of the concert was given over to the Black Watch, a regiment whose blue, black and green plaid kilts below red jackets had evoked great comment and mirth from the Provincials.

When they first marched out, in such impeccable formation that Mark realized he had never seen real marching before, they carried no instruments but a queer bag with sticks in it under the left arm.

"What's that?" he asked, poking Edward.

"Sssh. You'll find out."

Suddenly such a strange shrill conglomeration of sound split the night that Mark almost put his hands over his ears. It was like no other music, if it was music, and yet, gradually, it seemed to blend into his blood and heart and mind even more than the martial music of the regular band. When the end came, abruptly, he smiled shamefacedly at Edward. "I guess I must have some Scottish blood in me," he admitted. "The more I hear that the more I like it."

"They say it's an acquired taste," Edward grinned. "I like it now, but it took longer. But I'm just a bloody Sassenach, so I couldn't ever really appreciate it, I'm told."

The music, the marching, the whole atmosphere made Mark reluctant to return to his own quiet camp and hot shelter. "Let's look at the sap," he suggested. "I'd like to know just when your people are going to blow up that mine."

"So would everyone else, but McKellar's too canny a Scot to commit himself. There won't be much to see, but come on."

They followed the road through the woods toward the harbor. The pale light flooding under the branches showed the moon was larger than it had been at the fight at the village. They were nearing the ridge that ran from Morro Castle along the west shore of the harbor when the murmuring noises of the camp behind were split by the frenzied clamor of an iron bell and the sharp rattle of drums, both from the rear and above the castle. Muskets rattled and mortars boomed.

Edward grabbed Mark's arm. "That comes from the shore, ahead."

Another drum began to beat and suddenly men were streaming by, buckling belts, carrying ramrods and buckets of dirt.

"Get on there," shouted an officer. "All men to the shore."

"They're trying to relieve Morro," panted an officer as he raced by. "Get to the harbor batteries."

When they reached the batteries of mortars, that covered the castle though they could not dent the walls, someone thrust a musket, powder flask and bullet pouch at Mark from a stack by the road. The musket slipped naturally under his arm, the stock cool and hard to his hand.

"Fall in, men," a cool voice commanded. "Fall in. They landed by the waterside batteries and came up the hill. Carlton's coming."

Now Mark could distinguish the walls of Morro, high and to his right, and beyond the dark water of the harbor. Below the ridge on which he stood was a moving mass of men, white uniforms of the Spanish grenadiers in the center, dark figures spreading on either flank. Firing broke out to his left. He started to turn his head, but realized Edward was motionless beside him.

"They're attacking the 24-pounders," said a voice.

A tall officer, his gold braid black in the moonlight, strode by them. "I'm drawing the forward outposts back," he said, hardly raising his voice. "Fire at will and hold your line."

Mark gulped. "Who's that?"

"Colonel Carlton," whispered Edward.

The man on Mark's left raised his rifle, sighted and fired. Mark began to load. A ragged volley burst from the beach and he could hear the bullets whining overhead as he crouched. As his teeth tore at the paper covering the bullet Edward's musket went off and Mark nearly swallowed his bullet in surprise. His fingers seemed twice their normal size as he fumbled at the ramrod and then for his powder. There came another high volley. Men were tramping behind him and the mortars boomed steadily. "That's to keep the garrison from rushing out," he told himself, finding comfort in the thought. With the British and Provincial troops scattered over the several miles of the shore and the Cavannas, it would be long before reinforcements could reach this slope. If the Spanish landed in real force from the shore, and had another force to circle and attack by land, they could break over these thin lines of men and hurtle on to the entire camp. As he raised his musket he remembered Serafina and took careful aim into the straightening lines on the beach. The right flank was working down the shore to the south as though to flank the British line and take the guns from the rear. The center was forming to charge.

Suddenly the scrubby bushes on the hillside toward Morro glowed pink. "The royal battery," came a shout. "They got to it. They fired it."

The soldier on his left spat in the dust. "It'll burn three days."

"Why?" asked Mark around the next bullet.

"There's no water nor no sand to put it out. No dirt, and

what there is is too hard to dig. Never seen a country like it." The soldier fired in front meticulously. As Mark aimed again the mass of men seemed smaller.

"They're a crawling up the slope," said the soldier. "Carlton'll stop that."

A bugle rang. The soldier lowered his musket. "Prepare to charge. Got your sword?"

"Nooo," stammered Mark. He didn't know anything about swords.

The soldier turned for the first time and looked him over. "Gor blimey, a Provincial. And a blooming officer, too." He raised his voice. "Corp. If you're handing out swords, two more here."

A corporal, Mark could tell by the tassel that swayed on his left shoulder, moved up swiftly. "Wot you yelling for, Tweedy? You can't use three swords at once."

"It's for these two."

"Wot goes on . . ." the corporal began. Then he saw Edward. "Yessir. Didn't know we had an officer here." He raised his voice. "Here, you two, hand over yer swords."

"Quick," said Tweedy sharply. "We'll drive 'em. Nothing like our cold steel." His big fingers inserted the two bayonets expertly. "We let the first two lines through."

The bugle blared and ceased. Drums beat. The earth shook with the heavy tramp of feet that broke into a trot. The line of men where Mark stood began to move apart. Then big men, the biggest he had ever seen, trotted through the opened lines, their white trousers flashing past, their backs bent a little forward over the bayonets, a sudden solid, irresistible, moving wall. Another line followed, breaking into a steady lope as they passed over the ridge.

Then he himself was part of another line moving quickly down the low ridge.

It was uneven, rocky, sparsely spotted with small bushes. The British line in front was no longer straight. Some soldiers sprawled on the slope, some over rocks, but what was left was sweeping implacably towards the solid Spanish mass. Before that silent onward rush the mass suddenly gave way, breaking into small knots and groups that struggled with each other to run along the beach or vanish into the water. Some knots just stood still, their arms in the air. An officer called. The British line broke into three parts, the two outer sections wheeling to drive the Spaniards before them. Small boats were pushing from the shore.

Another command, and Mark's own line began to pace backward up the slope, bayonets still at ready. At the crest they halted, wheeled, and began to march back to camp. From the hillside to his left a mob of men were streaming inland. Some were soldiers, some seemed to be without uniform, some looked like negroes. The moonlight made things visible and yet veiled and unreal.

"Halt. Wheel. Fire over their heads."

Mark reached again for his bullet pouch. "Don't want no prisoners," muttered Tweedy. "We'd have to give the perishers water."

This time Mark was able to raise his musket and fire with the others. Then they grounded arms and stood impassively while the Spanish ran away. Ten minutes later they were marching to the parade ground and stacking muskets.

As they broke ranks Edward moved closer to Mark. "We better get out," he muttered. "We were ordered with the others, but someone might start wondering why we were there anyway."

They edged back from the open ground toward the road. Under a palm tree by a small fire an officer was lying on the ground. Another was kneeling, holding a canteen, while a man held the left arm.

"That's Carlton again," whispered Edward. "He won't like being wounded. He wants to be everywhere at once. Everyone says he's about our best officer, as intelligent as he is dashing and brave."

The road to the west was clear. Mark and Edward made their farewell gesture of a half salute and smile, and Mark set off on the long walk to his own camp. As he tramped he began to grin. He'd been under fire and he hadn't wavered or thought of being frightened. That was a good thing to have learned about himself.

16

Inside
Havana's
Walls

TALK and speculation flowed freely around the breakfast
fires the next morning. There were already several versions
of the night's attack, passed from one regiment to another,
and they all seemed wrong to Mark. He did not dare admit his share in the defense because he had been given leave
only for the regimental concert. The general opinion finally
was that the Spaniards had had a possible idea, that of attacking the thinly held ridge down from Morro, burning
the mortars that held the fort in siege while attempting a
flank attack down across the Cavannas to the sleeping regiments. But they apparently had counted on killing all the
sentries, and had failed in that. Then they had not had
sufficient courage, or leadership, though there were several
thousand men involved, to carry through the two attacks.
Someone had heard that many of the negro slaves had been
armed and made to fight, and Mark, remembering the dis-
organized masses flanking the Spanish soldiers, could believe that. There was some speculation as to whether another
flank attack might not be tried, for there were said to be
20,000 Spanish troops in Havana against the 4,000 regulars

from England and the 8,000 Provincials from North America. And Morro held 1,000 more. Another man had heard there were 50,000 armed slaves and guerillas, but he was laughed down. A flank attack through the woods of the Cavannas, or on the camp of Lord Howe across the bay at Chorrera, might be a very sticky business for the English. The final consensus was that any fight would be better than no fight, since they had come this far. By the end of an hour Mark's head was buzzing and he went back to the shelter to sleep.

In the afternoon a lanky provincial orderly came looking for Simon, who had gone with the water detail. Mark had noticed he went more often than ordered, and apparently held long conversations with Mama Hanno each time. The orderly allowed he wouldn't wait for Simon's return, and Mark offered to give any message.

"Jes' tell him Job Tucker come with his tail a-tween his legs," the man said in a nasal drawl. "Simon trusted me with two packets to put he knew where. Last night there was a mite of a dust-up, some Spaniards came messing and hollering around our lines, and we all went out to see what they had in mind. When I got back to Simon know's where, things were mussed up and one of those packets was gone. 'Tweren't Simon's, was t'other, with name Woodbridge on it. But I allowed Simon ought to know."

Mark managed to hold himself very still. "This was last night?" he asked carefully.

"Yup. 'Bout midnight. Wasn't a real fight, what might be called a diversion, to hold us down in case attack on Morro worked. Didn't amount to a hill of beans, no one hurt, but they took a prisoner."

Mark felt his breath catch. "Who?"

166

Tucker shrugged. "Don't know his name. Said to be a captain from over this way, New York they said, who'd come over with the water boats to see a friend in the 17th."

"Yes," said Mark. "It would be. Thanks. I'll tell Simon."

"Tell him to come over and visit." The leathery face creased in a near smile. "We'd figger some way to get the bar out of the cave. And tell him I'm real sorry about that packet. Weren't nothing else missing, though, so everything's all right." He nodded and strolled back towards the main camp.

Hot though the brush hut was, it was at least private. The men were sleeping, or just trying to sleep. Mark lay down. He had to think what to do next. There was no doubt it was Lamson who had taken his papers and gone off with the Spanish retreating from their feint. By simple reasoning he must have figured out where any valuable paper would be stowed, and then made the most of the given opportunity. So now he was in Havana with Pedro Peneranda. But there was no trust between them. Lamson might be holding on to the letter and will, bargaining all over again for his share. There was just one thing for Mark to do . . . get into Havana and the Casa Peneranda. And for that he needed Angelo. But Angelo usually came around supper time, to check on Mark's safety and run any errands and share whatever there might be to eat. Mark's impulse was to start for Havana immediately, but he sternly told himself not to be a fool. He would wait for Angelo, and for Simon, and in the meantime try to plan what he would do. But in his planning he fell asleep.

He awoke as the cooks were beating on the iron kettles to announce mess. He hurried out to find Simon, but no one had seen him.

"Etty?" Captain Olcott looked up from his bowl of pale soup. Mark noticed how thin and leathery his long face had grown over the past weeks. "Why, some men from the 9th came and wanted to go fishing and I sent Etty to show them how and where and told him he could go back to their mess afterwards."

Mark saluted stiffly. He couldn't wait. He'd have to go alone.

When Angelo appeared Mark fairly pulled him inside the hut. "I've got to go to Havana. Right away. Can you get your brother?"

Angelo looked solemn. "I go tell him now. Come back. Take you to him. He take you Casa Peneranda." Only when he had vanished did Mark realize the boy had had no supper.

Over the stew Tom Davidson embarked on a long, rambling tale about the time he had gone up to Hartford for his father and met a yellow-haired girl who kind of liked him but he forgot to ask her name and never could find her again. Mark heard one word out of ten. When he was through the stew he went and scrounged some food for Angelo and retreated to the hut.

It was black when Angelo returned with the same trousers and shirt, now clean and patched. "Brother wait," he whispered. "He not like it, but go because your friend save Hipico."

"Hipico?" Mark could not remember who Edward had rescued.

"Hipico name of burro," Angelo explained. "Hipico is meaning horse, big horse. Hipico is small burro, so we call him big horse to make him feel good. Hipico our burro."

Mark was ready. If only he could leave a message for Simon.

"I come back tell *El Señor* Etty," Angelo assured him as he helped push aside the upright branches that made the back wall of the hut. At the last minute Mark took the silver dagger from Simon's knapsack and stuck it in his belt. He remembered the feeling of having nothing to fight with, and in the city. . . . Once through the hut Angelo took Mark's hand and began to guide him confidently through the blackness, twisting and turning, until they came on the track that skirted Peralta. The smell of the houses that had been burnt still tainted the heavy air.

Here Roberto joined them, an almost invisible figure. "*Muy bueno*, Angelo," he whispered. "I Roberto, *Señor*. We walk to shore, take boat to warehouses. Is safer, quicker."

"*Vaya con Dios*," said Angelo softly. Mark felt silly as Roberto took his hand, but he realized he would be lost in a minute by himself. As they hurried down the cart track he asked, "Did you live at Casa Hermosa at the time of Don Diego?"

"*Si, Señor*. Is how I know English. But no talk. Night has ears."

Behind them the still-hidden moon was spreading its soft glow. Mark shivered. Perhaps he was trying his luck too far. He thought of the recruits and the guerillas and the outlaws and of the two armies. He had no business to be hurrying like this through the night toward a beleaguered city—and Pedro Peneranda.

They were going westward. To his right he could make out the bulk of the hills of the Cavannas, where, from the northern slope, the English batteries kept El Morro under fire. The path wound around woods and little rises and suddenly ran into the open and he could see the spreading harbor and faint lights of the city opposite.

The boat of Roberto turned out to be a small dugout canoe hollowed from a log, such as the Indians had made in the early days. It was narrow and tippy, but solid. Remembering how huge the bay had looked from the height by Morro, Mark was glad he was not skirting it on foot. Just once, at least, he wasn't walking all the way. It was odd to think that they could cross the harbor unchallenged, but of course there would be no English to question them because of the blocked entrance, and to Spanish eyes they would be two Cubans. Roberto crouched in the stern and sculled the boat with a twisting of the paddle quite different from the stroke Mark had learned one summer from a wandering Mohawk. It was silent and effective, and Mark watched so intently to see if he could catch the knack that he was startled when the boat slid up on a small beach. The smell of charred wet wood hung thickly in the air, and he remembered Edward had said the English had burned the houses outside the walls, those the Spaniards had left.

"The shipyards," murmured Roberto, pointing to long black ruins.

To the right, now showing gray in the misty moonlight, were the heavy squat walls of Havana. Low towers jutted out at regular intervals. Somewhere a sentry paced slowly.

"How'll we get over that?" Mark asked.

"First walk." And walk they did, between the walls and the ditch and the dried bed of the river the English had cut and diverted. The houses had all been fired, but those of stone still stood in gardens already tangled and overgrown.

170

Then the river bed turned sharply left. Beyond the sixth tower Roberto pushed open a gate in a wall. The house beyond had only gaping windows; the garden was a mass of sprawling bushes. From under one clump Roberto pulled a bundle of what looked like matting, tucked it under his arm, and left the garden. A turn to the right, and Mark found himself looking at a wide shallow ditch and the wall of Havana, solid, formidable.

"Soldiers there," Roberto pointed to round towers to the left and to the right. "But soldiers don't watch."

He ran down into the ditch and across to the shadow at the base of the wall. The bundle, unwound, turned into a small ladder of what felt like plaited grass. Mark fingered it doubtfully.

"Very strong. Hold big man," Roberto assured him.

From the base of the wall he brought out what looked like the rusty head of a small mattock, which he tied to a rope and then to the ladder. Running out a little from the wall, he hurled the object up and over the top. Mark gave it a tug. It was firmly caught. Roberto climbed it agilely, peered down from the top, and disappeared. Mark followed slowly, the narrow strands hurting his hands, sure that every sentry on the walls could see him and was reaching for a gun. Did they shoot spies or hang them?

The top of the wall was broad enough for two men to march abreast, between low parapets. Mark crossed at a crouch, found the ladder and followed it down. Below Roberto muttered *"Prisa."* From the base of the wall a rough open slope, as exposed to view as the top of the wall itself, ran down to a narrow street, walled on the far side. Roberto followed it and plunged into the darkness of an alley, running between walls. Mark let out the breath he seemed to have been holding for at least five minutes. A few steps and they stood in an arched gateway. Mark put out his hand and felt the cold iron of a grille. Roberto whistled three notes, paused, repeated two, then one.

Without a sound the grille swung back. Roberto held Mark in place and whistled one falling note. A faint rising note answered, and the two stepped through the archway. A murmur of two voices and Roberto was whispering, "Here Frederico. Major domo. He take you now."

"What? Wait." Mark whispered urgently, grabbing at the white shirt beside him. "Where you going?"

"Go back. Must take away ladder."

"How'll I ever get out?"

"Sssh. Frederico will help. *Adios.*" A stir of air, and the grille closed behind him.

"Come, *Señor* Mark." It was an older voice. "I will guide you." A thin dry hand closed on his. Mark moved forward. He had wanted to come to Havana. He was here.

Down the corridor the hand led him and into a cavernous kitchen, filled with the odors of years of cooking, where one lamp glowed faintly in a far corner. Now Mark could see his guide was indeed an old man, dressed in a black suit of knee breeches and a long coat, with a black ribbon tying back his white hair. He paused and peered up at Mark and nodded slowly.

"You are indeed from *Señor* T'ad. When Mama Hanno sent me word I could not believe. But now I see the same eyes, the same look. *Señor,*" he gave a little bow, "you are welcome. I could wish that I might welcome you to your own home, the Casa Hermosa."

"You know about the will?" asked Mark excitedly.

"But yes. For sixty years I served Don Diego, and *Señor*

T'ad, his honored friend, and who honored me by saying he was mine." One frail hand raised. "Do not tell me. I know from your friend, who told Mama Hanno, of his death."

Mark remembered the dagger and pulled it out. "But did you know that it was this that killed him?"

The two hands that took the dagger began to tremble. "No!" he said strongly, and looked at Mark. "You could say nothing but the truth," and his head drooped. One hand gripped the handle, then relaxed. "I will remember." He returned the dagger and Mark slid it again beneath his belt.

"And now, *Señor* Mark, how may I serve you?"

The words could have made Mark uncomfortable, since he was not used to being served by anyone, but the dignity of the thin figure and friendly calm of the aged face told him to accept the offer as it was made.

"Well." Now he was here Mark was not quite sure what to do next. "Who is in the house now?"

"Myself. Concepcion, the cook and Maria, the maid, asleep in their room. Don Pedro left quickly two hours ago on the heels of a messenger."

Mark let out a sigh. "Good. Then it shouldn't take long." He began to pick his words. "My uncle left me Don Diego's will and a letter. Both have been stolen from their place of safekeeping. There is in the letter a—a clue to something."

The white head nodded. "To the Peneranda Hoard."

Mark was surprised that he was not surprised. This man was one to trust. "Yes, and I must search for what that clue tells me before it falls into this Pedro's hands."

"But certainly. What do you seek?"

"The portrait of Don Diego."

"Then come with me." Frederico lighted two candles in

a branching holder and led a circle of wavering light across the kitchen, through a door into a high cavernous room with a massive table in the center. It was very like the dining hall at the Casa Hermosa. At one end was a massive fireplace. Above it Mark could discern a portrait in a heavy frame. Frederico gestured with the candles. "It hangs on pegs. It can be taken down."

Mark brought one of the heavy armchairs and found the stone mantelpiece wide enough to hold him. Gingerly he raised the portrait from the pegs, climbed down and carried it to the table. Frederico held the candles high. The picture was of a slim young man with an aristocratic narrow face and high forehead in a white uniform, the left breast covered with medals and orders. The dark eyes were melancholy and intelligent. There was a faint, disconcerting resemblance to Pedro Peneranda.

Frederico's hand shook a little. "A great gentleman," he said, in a voice as soft as a fading breeze.

Mark would have liked to look longer at the face of the man who had been Uncle Thad's great friend, but he must hurry. The frame was dark and carved with fruit and flowers. Quickly he began to twist each one. Uncle Thad had only said that the unusual frame was worth particular attention. None of the fruit or flowers could be moved. He turned the picture on its face. But the wood at the back was solid and could not be loosened. Panic began to rise within him. There must be something. . . . Instead of twisting he began to press the rounded plums and cherries from one side and another and to try to slide the leaves. And then, at the bottom right-hand corner, a single cherry did move beneath his hand. He pushed again, and the carved fruit slid back just far enough to show a small cavity and a piece of paper. Frederico drew in his breath with a gasp. "*E verdad*," he whispered.

Gently Mark drew out the paper and held it toward the light. It was heavy paper, and quite blank on both sides.

He looked at Frederico. "Has someone else found the real paper?" His voice was hoarse and shaking with disappointment.

"That I cannot say. But it is greatly to be doubted."

Mark thrust the paper into the pocket of his breeches and slid the carved cherry back in place. More than ever he must hurry now. He must not let himself think of the end of his hopes and his mission. He carried the portrait back to the fireplace and hung it again. Now to get back to camp. It would be hard to tell Simon it had all been in vain.

"I hear someone," whispered Frederico. "I go. Stay quiet." He and the candles moved from the room toward the hall.

Mark pushed the armchair back in place. The windows on one side were high and grilled. No escape there. He started toward the door; the kitchen would be safer than here. Light appeared in the corridor, coming nearer.

17

The
Blank Paper

"BRING some wine and cold meat," a voice was saying. "I will eat now. But I will need more wine later."

Into the room strode the man who had called himself Pedro Galvez and who was Pedro Peneranda. Behind him, carrying a six branch candelabrum, came the thickset, squat man who had been at the Casa Hermosa that hot afternoon. Frederico followed, his face expressionless but his eyes anxious. A third man took up a position inside the door.

At sight of Mark, Pedro halted. "So? What have we here. A peon? Gaspar, bring that light."

They were all between him and the door. Mark stood still. Gaspar moved forward, holding the light high so it fell full on Mark's face.

"And so!" Surprise mingled with pleasure was in Pedro's exclamation. "It is the young Mark Woodbridge of Connecticut. Well, what have you to say?"

"I came to see the house where my uncle had lived," Mark managed to say calmly.

"Yes? And in disguise into a town that is under siege?"

The purring voice snapped suddenly. "Do not take me for a fool, young man. You came for what?"

"But this is the *soldado* who came to the Casa," cried Gaspar. "But let me at him."

"You would like that, for he caused you a beating." Beneath the yellow light the long face with its black eyes seemed suddenly to spring at Mark. The shadows made the forward thrusting narrow head as vicious as a snake's. "So you do seek something! Gaspar, put the light on the table and search him."

Pedro unfastened the long black cloak he was wearing and Frederico took it from his shoulders. "Wine, Frederico, and meat, as I said."

"*Si Señor*," murmured Frederico, and left without a glance at Mark.

Mark could not take his eyes from the white face with its baleful eyes, even while Gaspar pulled the dagger from his belt and the white paper from his pocket. Both were tossed on the table. "That is all, *Señor*."

Pedro picked up the paper, looked at it. "Bah, a blank paper. What game is this?" He crumbled it and tossed it to one side. Mesmerized though he was, Mark could see that it fell beneath a chair at one side of the door. The dagger Pedro held for a moment. "So. You brought it with you." He tossed it on the table. "Childish." He stepped nearer Mark. "And now you will tell me why you are here."

The eyes held little dancing points of light from the candles. Mark could see nothing else. Deep inside himself he knew he was afraid as he had never been afraid, and was behaving like a coward. But he could not move while those eyes were on him. He wet his lips. "Nothing," he mumbled. It was the best he could do.

"But you will tell me, you know. It is better to tell without being forced to tell."

Mark could only stare.

"Gaspar, Carlos, throw him."

The next thing Mark knew, he was lying sideways on the floor, both arms jerked up behind his back and Carlos astride him.

"Hold him, Carlos. You have your little knife, Gaspar?"

"*Si, Señor,* as always," answered Gaspar eagerly. "The eyes?"

Mark's arms were jerked even higher until he almost cried out with the pain.

"No, no. Not yet. Woodbridge, what did you come for?"

Now that he was no longer confronted by that venomous face Mark could shake his head. "Nothing," he mumbled again.

"Very well. You will learn. Gaspar, the little finger first."

The point of a knife went into the end of his finger and he felt himself go limp.

"Bah," said the voice, whirling above him. "They are soft, the *Americanos*. He has fainted."

"Another finger will bring him out, *Señor*," Gaspar offered.

"Later. We will wait for my friend, who would wish to be here. And I wish to eat, and not to be disturbed while I do. Carry him to the cellars."

Mark felt himself lifted roughly by the two men. He was carried into the hall and down some steps to a place that smelled musty and damp. The hands carrying him let him drop suddenly. His head hit stone.

It was the blackest blackness he had ever seen. What was it? Panic shook him. In spite of his throbbing head he pushed himself upright. His finger was throbbing, and when he touched it he found it covered with blood. But he must find out what this place might be. At the third try he could stand erect. With hands outstretched he began to feel his way.

He was in a small room, six paces by four, absolutely bare, made of massive stone. There was a door of heavy wood, and that was all. He leaned against the wall. What could he do? Not counting Frederico, there were three men, and another coming. He had no weapons. And even if he could get out of the Casa he was in an enemy city, in disguise, with no idea how to get out. He shook himself. He *must* think of something.

What was it Pedro had said? Yes. They were going to question him again, when the other man came. Would Pedro send one man or two to fetch him? He thought of Pedro Peneranda and shivered. All his life he would remember that white face, those terrifying eyes. If only he would not have to see it again! But if he kept thinking of that he would never do anything. And he must. Other men had been caught, locked up. What had they done to escape? He forced his mind back to tales he had heard. *Yes!* There was one old trick. Would these men be careless enough for it to work? He moved over and felt the door. There was no crack, nothing for any purchase. He took off his left shoe and waited.

He had no idea how long he waited until a key began to turn and the door moved slowly open. There was just enough light from the corridor to see the heavy figure of

Gaspar as he stopped inside the door to peer into the cell. From behind the door Mark sprang forward and brought the heavy heel of the shoe against the side of the man's head. Gaspar gave a grunt and staggered. Mark hit him, on the temple, with all his might. As Gaspar fell Mark darted to the doorway. The corridor was empty. One candle burned in a sconce high on the wall. Keeping his shoe at hand, Mark pulled the belt from the inert figure and tied the man's ankles, and the wrists with a cotton kerchief from one pocket. He put on his shoe, closed and locked the door behind him. It was a big key that weighed down his pocket, but it might be useful.

The passageway was low; the steps at one end shallow and narrow. Mark crept upward. He must get back that paper, blank though it was. Perhaps there had been pinpricks in a pattern he had missed. Even if it held nothing, there might be some clue as to whether it was the one left by Uncle Thad. The stairs came out by a storeroom, from the smell, and next was the kitchen. There were lights in the hall. From the door into the *sala* came a crack of light and voices.

Standing well back from the slit he could see that two massive candelabra holding six candles each shone on the polished table, white plates and napkins and two goblets of red wine. At the head of the table sat Pedro, leaning back in the high-backed chair. Behind it stood Frederico, napkin over one arm. By shifting a little Mark could see a man in a dark coat in a chair at the right. As he half turned to pick up his wine glass Mark saw it was Captain Lamson.

"But I am not sure I approve of your using my name, my dear Captain," Pedro was saying icily.

"Couldn't think of any other way to get those stupid

soldiers to let me go. I'd have been here last night, if it hadn't been for them. The raid was well managed, but I lost my way, as I told you, somewhere between the camp and the city, and a corporal's guard picked me up. I tried to send for you then, but they were too excited and wouldn't listen. Couldn't get hold of an officer until this afternoon, and then he wouldn't believe I knew you until you came and convinced him." His voice grew angry. "You could have brought me back in your carriage. I don't like walking."

"But it would not have been wise to be seen further with you," Pedro purred gently. "Be satisfied you are no longer in that hut, a prisoner. And, speaking of prisoners, I have one of my own."

Lamson took another swallow of wine and began to eat quickly. Frederico stepped forward, filled the glass, and retreated.

"Who's that?" the Captain asked indifferently.

"The young Mark Woodbridge. He came here, alone."

"Here? He's on to something."

"So I believe. And, since he is alone and in disguise, we may treat him as a spy—or as we wish."

"Yes. Mmmm. Wonder what . . ."

"We will soon know. I have sent Gaspar to bring him here."

"Thought you had another man."

"Carlos is patrolling around the Casa, in case the young man should try to escape, or anyone should come to interrupt us." He sipped the wine. "You have the papers?"

Lamson slapped the pocket of his coat. "Safe here. Though I'm not saying it was easy, getting them from Old Put's own strong box in the middle of his camp."

The black eyes widened. "But of course I knew of your skill, my dear Captain." One white hand stretched across the table. "I will see them."

Lamson drew away. "When you pay me. And in English pounds, as you agreed. And also the pounds you promised when I took word of any English plans into Morro."

Pedro waved a languid hand. "In that I merely acted for Don José Entrada. You will have to get the five hundred pounds from him."

"That isn't what you said in New York. Who's he?"

"The Governor of Cuba." And Pedro laughed.

Lamson sat quite still. "So you gulled me on that one? You won't on the other."

The hand flicked back. "I'll pay, when I know what they are worth. And of course we may not need them, when the young man begins to talk."

"Oh, you'll need them all right. It's the will you want above all, isn't it?"

"You understand so well, dear Captain."

"You also want that treasure, the Peneranda Hoard." Lamson leaned back again. "Well, bring out young Woodbridge. But he doesn't know where it is."

"He will come. Gaspar is probably amusing himself for a few minutes." The sleek black head turned. "Frederico, you may go. We will need you no longer."

Frederico bowed and walked down the long room toward the door.

"Aren't you afraid he knows too much?" Lamson asked curiously.

"No." The voice was indifferent. "He was my uncle's major domo. He is devoted to the family. And now,

Captain, we will settle the price of the will, and any other document there may be."

Frederico stepped through the door and closed it behind him. Mark stood motionless in the shadow. The old man, looking more bent and tired than before, moved slowly towards the center of the room and beckoned. "Come, *Señor* Mark. I will guide you out."

Mark walked towards him. "Why should I trust you?" he asked hoarsely.

Frederico gave him a tired wisp of a smile. "Why? For the sake of *Señor* T'ad. And, see, I have brought you these."

From a pocket he pulled the crumpled paper and the silver dagger. Mark seized them. "Thank you," he said humbly. "I shouldn't have doubted. . . . How did you know I would get out?"

"I prayed. Against Gaspar I myself could do nothing . . ." the old hand made a gesture, "but you are young, strong . . . Gasper is in the cell?"

Mark nodded as he pushed the paper to the bottom of his pocket.

"Then come."

With the small candlestick held high he turned toward the storeroom. At the foot of the steps he halted. "You have the key of the cell? I will leave it by the door. I would not condemn even Gaspar to such a death, for the door cannot be broken down, or otherwise opened."

When he returned he faced the narrow section of stone wall at the left of the steps, pushed in two places, and the wall swung out. He smiled at Mark's amazement. "A passage, *Señor*. Don Diego knew, but now I, alone, know. It was built by Don Diego's father, for many purposes. It takes us beyond the walls. Come."

As they stepped into the narrow darkness the door closed.

"Can you open it again?" Mark asked anxiously.

"Surely. And *Señor* Pedro will think I have gone to my room. If you fear for me, do not. He will never harm me, for he knows my family, which is large, would not let him live long if he did."

The rock-lined passage dipped down, ran straight until it rose again to a blank wall above some steps.

"Here one pushes," murmured Frederico. "Alone I could not."

Mark set his back against the block. At the third heave it began to move. Slowly it rose until it stood at right angles. The damp night air rushed about them. The moonlight was dazzling. Mark looked down at Frederico standing below him.

"Let down the stone gently," said the soft voice. "Roberto awaits you by the house. Go, *Señor* Mark. I am at last happy now that I have seen the nephew of *Señor* T'ad."

Mark backed down the steps and held out his hand. "Thank you, Frederico, for everything. When the Casa Hermosa is mine, I will hope you will come and be my major domo."

A ghostly smile came to the white face. "That may not be. But from Angelo I will hear of you. I will pray for justice, and for you. *Vaya con Dios*, young *Señor*." The fragile hand touched Mark's. He wanted to say something more, but the right words would not come. "Thank you," he said gently, "and, and take care of yourself."

As he eased the stone back into place he had a last glimpse

of the old face smiling up at him from beneath the feeble candle.

Mark straightened and looked around. He was standing at one side of the paving that surrounded an empty pool. The white house ahead looked familiar: it was the one where Roberto had found the ladder. Beside the same clump of bushes he found Roberto, asleep.

"*Señor*," he breathed, as Mark woke him. "I am glad. We must go. Quickly."

Mark felt tired in every bone of his body. His head still ached. It did not seem possible he had been inside Havana and now was outside the walls. "I'll go as quickly as I can," he mumbled.

"Must get across harbor," Roberto explained, and trotted toward the shipyards. In the boat Mark buried his head in his hands. All these weeks, everything, had been for a blank piece of paper. Something must have happened to the other. Uncle Thad wouldn't play a joke. In dull despair he followed Roberto back to the hut.

18

El Morro
Is Stormed

"INSPECTION in an hour," Simon called, coming back to the hut from water duty. "Something's up with the Britishers. Clean your musket. Angelo's working on our boots."

There was an air of excitement over the company street as men brushed dusty uniforms, polished buckles and swabbed muskets. Old Put was coming to inspect, the first time they'd seen him since the landing. Perhaps there'd be a fight yet.

But Old Put just stalked up and down the lines without a word, spoke briefly to the Captain and marched westward.

"He didn't look at anything," complained Tom Davidson. "And I got my musket as clean as a newly laid egg."

"He's mad. That means we don't get to fight," opined Nat.

"Break ranks," called Olcott, and the men crowded around to hear the news. "The British are blowing up their mines and storming Morro," he went on conversationally. There was a faint cheer.

"Are we going to help?" called someone.

"Do we get to go home tomorrow?" asked another.

Olcott frowned. "No to both. They say they'll attack without us. If the attack fails the siege goes on."

"Who's going to do the fighting?"

"The 9th is leading the assault on the castle, with a battalion of the Royal Americans, one of the Morgans, and the 90th from Belle Isle in support. We have permission to go watch." His voice was neutral.

"Nice of them," muttered Nat.

"Well, at least they're doing the fighting," said Mark quickly. He was thinking of Edward, who had hoped for a fight. He would have liked to tell his friend to take care of himself, but he realized that was just not done.

"Come on," said Simon. "We got to get a place with a good view."

The thick underbrush of the Cavannas plateau had been still farther cleared away back from the fort to give the besieging batteries a clear line of fire. Their intermittent boom had become an accepted and then unnoticed part of the background of the camps. Like the guns of the fleet, the shore batteries had been unable to make any dent in the massive walls of the castle. Now the bare hillside was covered with men, the sober brown coats of the Provincials the only dark note amid the moving mass of red and white.

As Mark looked from the plateau to the fort he realized they were too far away to see the north side of the bastion where the mine lay and where the assault would follow the explosion. With Simon he began to head toward the shore. The morning was hot and clear, and the air was charged with excitement. Officers stood in clusters talking, but their eyes, with those of the soldiers, were turned to the fort and the red and yellow flag floating above it. At

187

last, they all were saying to themselves, at last something is going to happen. From them all rose a low steady hum as of an enormous hive of bees. Near the big moat the regiments that would make the assault were already armed. Mark looked eagerly for Edward, but with three regiments behind the 9th there was no chance of seeing him.

"We'd get a good view from those trees," Simon said, pointing to a grove that had been left to shield an officer's tent.

The oak-like trees were not high, but from a branch twenty feet up Mark found he did indeed have a good view of the bastion, ditch and fort. Some officers moved toward the waiting lines. A single drum beat a soft roll. Along the ramparts of the fort a line of bayonets caught the sun in sharp points of light. Black guns stood in the embrasures.

"Why don't they fire at us?" Mark asked.

"Can't get the cannon muzzles down far enough. Never thought they'd be attacked by land here. But you'd think with all the powder and shot they've got in there they'd shoot anyway, as the crow said to the hunter."

A group of officers was walking slowly toward the moat. Mark wondered if the Scottish engineer did really have enough powder to blow up a hole in that grim fortress. He wondered how Edward felt.

The officers moved with quick precision back from the edge of the moat. Simon clapped his hands to his ears and ducked his head. "Hold tight. Here it comes."

Mark gripped the tree trunk, the rough bark biting into his fingers.

With a roar greater than when the ice broke in the Connecticut in the spring a black cloud billowed upward. It spread wide, hiding the moat and the walls of the fortress, mounting into the blue sky. All was silence, as though the thousands of men were holding their breath, until a deep crashing rumble filled their ears. The rumble groaned into its own silence which was followed by a light pattering as of rain. Mark looked up, and ducked. Tiny rocks were showering down through the trees, tearing the leaves. But the lines of soldiers had not quivered beneath the hail of stones.

The black smoke rolled above the fort. The wind caught it, shredded it, and carried it westward. Now the walls were lined with heads as well as bayonets. A faint shouting drifted down to the immobile ranks below. Now it could be seen that the outermost mine, near that narrow rock wall by the shore, had only brought down a pile of rock from the cliff itself. The strong walls of Morro stood undamaged.

A short bark of a cheer, quickly cut off, made Mark look inland to the bastion. He almost cheered himself, for this mine had both brought down some of the rock face of the cliff and had blown a narrow breach in the wall of the bastion itself. Mark scrambled one branch higher, bending the treetop with his weight. Yes, there was a long narrow hole in the wall above a mound of still-falling rubble.

Simon shook his head. "Not good enough," he proclaimed from his perch. "Too narrow. Need another mine, and that'll mean more weeks waiting."

For five minutes nothing happened. Then came the shrill call of fifes and the steady rat tat of a drum. The first red lines moved, formed into marching order, and advanced up the slope to the edge of the ditch until a rattle of drums halted them.

"They're in musket range of the walls!" cried Mark. "They could all be shot right there."

Simon broke a twig and began to chew it. "Slaughter," he muttered, "fair slaughter."

A bugle fluted a call. A file of soldiers detached itself from the lines, marched to the edge of the moat and disappeared into it, one by one. There came a volley and white puffs of smoke. The heads and bayonets above the walls disappeared.

"That covering fire means they'll attack," exclaimed Simon. "But they can't, through that hole. It'll take only one man at a time!"

Bugle and drum joined together. Two files of the 9th dressed ranks. An officer stepped out to place himself at their head. The files faced seaward and began to march forward.

"To get to that breech they've got to cross on that wall of rock," Simon pointed, "and it's only wide enough for one man."

"They can't attack Morro one at a time," Mark gasped. "But they are."

The soldiers turned at right angles and mounted the slope. Two more ranks, led by an officer, were following. At the edge of the moat the first two files dressed again, and faced seaward. Their guns on their shoulders, bayonets shining, they followed the officer along the brink of the moat, turned at right angles, and began, one at a time, to follow across the curtain of rock, balancing a little because of the narrowness. Across the moat they faced left to clamber up the pile of rock that led to the narrow split in the walls.

A muffled volley came from within the fort, then, clearly,

from one of the angles of the star-shaped bastion. The four soldiers on the rock wall hesitated. The one nearest the fort pushed a foot forward, leaned over slowly and rolled out of sight. The three others bent their knees, and still holding their muskets, disappeared into the moat below. The soldiers following did not even turn their heads to watch their comrades. In their turn they moved across the wall. Another volley, and the four, bending as easily as rag dolls, fell. The line never paused. One by one it advanced briskly, implacably. A third volley and only one man fell.

Mark turned to the breech. The officer was at the wall. His arm moved, his sword flashing in the sunlight. He stepped forward to squeeze his way through the slit. The soldier behind him followed closely, and the next and the next. The line of red and white was moving steadily in spite of the now ragged fire.

"By the great horned spoon," Simon cried, "if them Spanish don't fight to hold a fort when men come at 'em one by one they don't deserve to hold this, nor Havana, nor anything else."

Almost at his words muffled cheering rose from behind the walls. The yellow and red flag gave a jerk not caused by the wind, then, slowly, slowly, began to drop towards the earth. Mark found himself trying to stand and cheer. It couldn't happen so quickly! The flag disappeared. The only sound was the rattle and fall of a dislodged rock. Something red showed against the sky. Swiftly it flew up the pole, caught the breeze, and spread triumphantly. From the plain, from the hillside, from the whole camp came the hoarse roar of a cheer that rivaled any cannonade.

As it died away Mark saw Simon wipe his forehead with the back of his hand. "I was sweating there with the boys for a bit," he admitted wryly. "Show's over now." He began to climb down his tree.

Mark found to his surprise his breath was still coming in short jerks. He had seen a long chance magnificently taken and magnificently succeed. He knew he would never forget that single line of men in red and white crossing the wall, mounting the gray face of the rock, obeying orders and the call of duty from the bugle.

"Quite a sight," allowed Simon, jerking his thumb toward the soldiers, the guns, the tents, the officers, the fort. "But I don't hold by it. War's really too dang much trouble."

19

A Call
on Colonel Putnam

FOR some never-explained reason there was more beef in
the stew pot than usual. Each soldier squatted around the
kettles had his own news, opinions and views. Mark
laughed inside. How true it was that if you took a hundred
Connecticuters and showed them the same tree you'd have
a hundred different opinions about it.

"Now we got Morro, won't be long before we have
Havana," Simon started off.

"There's that Punta on the other side of the harbor."

Simon snorted. "Nothing to that. And Howe's got so
many regulars and grenadiers and colonials they could just
walk over it by plain weight."

A man from Torrington wagged his head. "But half of
what Howe's got are down sick. And there's walls to the
city. And all them armed slaves out in the hills."

"Soon's we got Punta we can heist out them ships block-
ing the harbor, and the fleet can sail in and say it'll bombard the town, and there won't be any more fighting at all,
at all."

"I heard more'n that," volunteered Tom between earnest

chews. "I heard that 3,000 more troops came in from New York two days ago. They're over with Howe. They can walk over Punta and Havana, if the rest're sick."

Nat brightened. "More provincials? They've got too many now. P'raps they'll start sending us home."

"It's them from the islands, Guadiloupy and Martiniqy that'll get to go first, cause they're nearer and it'd be quicker."

A solemn nodding of heads agreed with this sad view.

"We'll get to go soon," Simon told them cheerfully. "And we saw this morning what the Britishers mean when they talk of discipline and doing things the hard way. They'd rather do things their way than ours, no matter how hard." He scraped the bottom of his panikin and kicked Mark. "Want to go fishing anyone?" he asked lazily.

Mark rose reluctantly as the others grunted dissent. He felt he would rather do anything than sit in the sun and fish, but Simon had produced lines and hooks and they set off for the redoubt at a quick trot.

The redoubt of Coximar was gray and squat and square with a triangular bastion at each corner. The north corner over the low cliff side was where one fished, but Simon led the way to the box-like structure in the center and stretched in the shade on the eastern side. Mark felt there wasn't much difference between the shade and the sun at any time, but sat down beside him.

"Tell me what happened in Havana," directed Simon, and Mark told his tale, from the first news of the packet missing from Putnam's strong box to the dragging return with Roberto.

Simon scratched one leg thoughtfully. "Ummm. You were lucky, as the bull said to the peddler as he cleared the fence. It'll all bear thinking about later. But this paper, now. You got it?"

"Yes, but it's either one of Uncle Thad's jokes, or it's been put there by someone else."

"Thad was too much a Connecticuter to joke about something serious like money. T'other's possible. Let's see the paper."

Mark thrust his hand deep into the pocket of his breeches and pulled out the heavy, crumpled white paper. Simon spread it on his knee and looked at first one side and then the other.

"What did Thad write you about it?"

As Mark shook his head despondently Simon's voice sharpened. "Snap to, boy. You said once you could recollect every smitch of that letter he left you. Think back, now, slow like."

Mark closed his eyes and tried to see the letter. "He wrote that I must always keep the picture of Don Diego. That I would find it had a very unusual frame. That if he was not there to show me I must find a piece of paper that would tell me what I need to know, after I remember a trick he showed me."

Simon flung out a hand. "There. You recollected that. Now, what did Thad ever show you about a piece of paper?"

"I can't remember a thing." Mark put his head in his hands. "He wrote a letter . . ." His voice trailed away miserably as Simon snorted. He squeezed his eyes tighter. Of course there was something. After a moment's silence he dropped his hands. "I can't remember anything else."

"Bah, boy, that's no use." Simon unfolded his legs and stood up. It was the first time Mark had ever seen him give a sign of temper, and he could only watch with astonishment as Simon stalked toward the parapet, anger in every line of his thin figure. But when he came back his face was as expressionless as usual.

"Shouldn't blame you for not remembering everything," he said gently. "No one can do that. Let me see the paper. And keep quiet."

He ran his finger over the surface on both sides, shook his head, and held the paper up to the light. "No pinpricks," he muttered. "I've heard tell of that. And it's too thin to be split and something put inside." He got up again and walked to the parapet. Mark followed.

Below them lay the steep brown rocks above the blue water. Some broken leaves and sticks, a piece of torn cloth, a dead fish that had flopped from the hook, showed the soldiers had been fishing again. In a crevice two round sour oranges like the boys sometimes brought from the village looked like yellow forest toadstools.

Simon pounded the stone with his fist. "There must be something." He leaned across the parapet and looked at the trees on the opposite point, the water, the rocks below. He stiffened. "Might be," he half whispered, "worth trying, as the snake said as it tried to swallow the hen's egg. Mark, go fetch some sticks and tinder."

They made a fire in the corner of the bare guard room, the darkest place Simon could find, and waited until the first darting flames had died down to a glow. Mark had opened his mouth three times to ask questions and each time had shut it again at Simon's expression. Simon held the paper in front of the fire, so close Mark almost snatched it back to safety. Nothing happened.

"Get more wood," Simon ordered sharply.

196

This time the glow from the coals was brighter. As Simon held the paper so closely his hands reddened from the heat, brown scattered letters in Uncle Thad's small handwriting slowly grew from the paper. When the lines showed complete Simon's leathery face relaxed in a smile. "Nothing like a try that works, as the bear said as he knocked over a bee tree. Read it, Mark, you're used to Thad's writing."

"If you read this you are alone," Mark began slowly. "Perhaps Beltran is also gone. It will mean all is not well. But the jewels are still there, I know, and they are yours. Two miles east of Casa Hermosa, still on Peneranda land, there is a shallow bay. At the southwest corner of this bay there is a dry stream that has left a bed filled with boulders and rocks. Go up the west side to where three boulders lean to form a tent. Behind the inner one, near the edge of the bank, is a flat stone. This must be raised. Beneath is the chest that holds the Peneranda Hoard. On top you will see a little leather bag; this holds my own small treasure. Of the Peneranda, give to Beltran what you wish for himself and for those he commends for faithful service. This is the wish of Don Diego and myself. The rest is yours to use, but use it wisely. T.B."

They sank back on their heels, and the dark writing faded slowly.

"Be switched," ejaculated Simon. "It *is* there."

"How'd you know about the writing?" Mark gasped.

"Didn't know. Just guessed. But I'll have to allow I wouldn't of if it hadn't been for them oranges. They're kind of yellow, and I wondered if they were oranges or lemons, and it was lemons did it. Heard tell once of sending a message through the lines written in lemon juice. When juice dries it don't show—hold it to the fire it comes out.

Simple when you know how, as the owl said as it caught a mouse."

"I remember now," Mark broke in. "Uncle Thad did show me about the writing, with a lemon he brought special from New Haven. But it was late at night at haying time and he talked a lot and I was sleepy and I didn't pay much attention to what he was saying or doing. I remember I went to sleep before he was finished and he put me to bed and said he'd show me again, but he never did."

"No wonder you didn't recollect it," Simon said comfortingly. "He must have thought you were more awake than you were. Now we ought to get hold of this Beltran before we go after that chest."

"But we don't need to go after it," Mark pointed out. "It's on my land. We can just wait until we take Havana, and then I can go to the Governor and claim the Casa Hermosa. Ohhhh." He stopped. "I forgot. I don't have the will any more." He stared at the dying fire so Simon would not see his desolation.

Simon looked at him obliquely. "That's as may be. Perhaps that Lamson didn't split with that Pedro after all. We'll mosey over with one of the water boats and see Job and perhaps Old Put himself. He might have some good, hardheaded advice for us. No one's harderheaded than Old Put, as the Indians found out." Suddenly he chuckled.

"All right, but I don't see much use," Mark agreed hopelessly. "But, anyway, there's no hurry about getting the Hoard. No one else knows where it is."

"Put that paper in your belt," Simon ordered. "We'll remember, but it's best to keep it. And we better get us some fish so's no one'll suspicion we've been using our time other ways."

The assault on the fort, the death of the Spanish commander who had died of wounds received when trying to defend his flag, the number of the soldiers captured, and the number drowned trying to escape by swimming across the harbor, were discussed so endlessly that afternoon that Mark decided to go and see Edward. He'd have some peace and quiet on the walk over, at least.

Edward was watching his orderly pipe-clay his white gaiters, and grinned when he saw Mark. "Glad you came. Here, I'll put on the other pair, Bates. Colonials don't like to wait for anything, even fresh gaiters."

As they strolled toward the shore Mark told him of the admiration all had felt for those unflinching soldiers who had taken the fort.

"I didn't get up to the breech myself until it was almost all over," Edward admitted ruefully. "And by then there was only a little more fighting. But, yet, it was something to have done."

It made Mark proud to be English himself when he looked at the narrow breech, the grim fortress, and the red flag whipping in the breeze. He couldn't quite put it in words, but he clapped Edward on the back, and that seemed to say it all.

As they wandered back through the camp of the sappers and then along the road through the woods, Mark told of his adventure in Havana and the message on the paper, and his decision to wait until Cuba was English-held before he did anything more.

"But," Edward exclaimed, "you may not have the time you think."

"Lots of time," Mark assured him grandly.

Edward shook his head. "It's only a rumor I heard at

mess. But in an army many rumors often turn out to be true," he added in a grown-up way that made Mark smile. "It is said that since 3,000 more troops have come down from the Colonies, the first of the Provincial troops here will be sent back in the same ships."

"When?" Mark asked incredulously.

"When the ships are watered and ready. It is felt that so many troops will not be needed, now, to take the city and the island. There's little spirit left in the Spanish, our spies tell us, and the siege of the city will not be long, particularly as they, too, are short of water. Soon we can bombard the city, for La Punta fell today. And the Council felt the first Provincials to reach here should be the first to return home again."

Mark sat down on a boulder. "But *we* were the first . . . That means I won't have a chance to see the Governor . . . or anything."

"But, perhaps in a year you could come back," Edward suggested sympathetically. "And there is still a day or so, I am sure. We will think of something. And if you want any help in—er—anything, let me know."

Mark shook his head. "I don't see what we can do."

It was as he started to tell Simon the rumor that he first noticed a new bare-legged urchin who was trying to stand closer and closer to them. The boy had a squeezed-up face and a squint in one eye. Mark dropped his voice, and noticed the boy moved nearer.

"*Vamos*," ordered Simon quietly. The boy moved a little. "Angelo," Simon raised his voice. "That boy. Make *vamos*."

"*Si, Señor, con gusto*," Angelo answered from the door of the hut.

"Who's he?" Mark asked, as Angelo returned, beaming, from chasing the boy through the brush.

"Tomás, *Señor*. He has come to the Casa Hermosa with the men who have returned. He said he just wanted to see the camp. But not a good boy, like me." He went back happily to polishing Simon's musket.

At the report of the rumor Simon chewed his underlip thoughtfully. "Can't say I'll be sorry to see Connecticut again, but I sure hate to leave something unfinished. And you won't have a chance of snow in August of getting your Casa once we leave. We'll go see Old Put tomorrow. I'll fix it up, and have a talk with Mama Hanno, too. I wouldn't be surprised if she isn't a *bruja*, after all."

"What's that?" Mark wasn't interested. All Uncle Thad had tried to do for him, all this soldiering, and for nothing.

"A *bruja's* a witch. She sure knows everything that goes on, anyway. Cheer up, boy. It isn't over yet."

The thought of actually facing Colonel Putnam and trying to convince that formidable figure of an incredible story made Mark feel weak at the knees. He went over and over his story for most of the evening, to try to make it short. The more he told it to himself the more impossible it sounded, particularly as he had no evidence except the silver button and the silver dagger. There was the page of directions from Uncle Thad, but anyone could say he'd forged it himself. If only he had the will! That was impressive, if unreadable. If only the Colonel didn't get irritated or bored. And there was the problem of Captain Lamson. Perhaps he better not mention him by name. The bed of branches had never felt harder or more filled with penetrating knobs and points, as he wiggled to find a smooth spot.

Simon had arranged for passage on the water boats from the Rhode Island company on the promise they'd both take an oar each way. It was just sunrise when they pulled away to the west, past the British camp, the castle, the harbor entrance with the walls and roofs of the city shining across the lightening water, the flat land that held over half the army and the mouth of the Chorrea river. At any other time Mark would have enjoyed seeing it all, but he could only think of the interview ahead. Assured it would take at least two hours to fill the casks, because of the other companies, Simon trotted briskly around the camp of Howe's grenadiers toward that of the Provincials. The sun was now well up, and the day already hot.

"Won't we be too early to see the Colonel?" Mark asked nervously. "How do we know he'll see us anyway?"

"If he's in the right temper, and not busy, he'll always see his men. He'll never get too toplofty for that. 'Sides, we've fought together; he won't forget that. And 'sides we have Job to fix it."

Putman's tent was no larger than that of the other officers, and its only advantage was the scanty shade of two palm trees. He was sitting in front of it, alone, eating from a panikin just like Mark's.

"Let him finish," muttered Simon. "We'll find Job."

Job was making tea over a small fire at one side. "Mornin'," he nodded, as casually as though they'd seen each other the day before. "Not good mornin'," he added, " 'cause no mornin's good here. Colonel, he don't like it, neither."

"Could we have a few words with him?" Simon asked easily.

Job cocked his leathery face to one side, and reminded Mark again of a scrawny rooster. "Let him get halfway through his tea, then come." He poured a nearly black liquid into a pewter mug and hacked some sugar off a loaf on the ground, nodded, and stalked around the tent. The two waited until they saw him jerk his head. The mug was half empty when they stood before the Colonel.

"You recollect Simon Etty, Colonel." Job's flat voice made Mark homesick again. "Him and his friend want to see you for a minute."

Simon stiffened to attention. Mark did his best, but his stomach felt hollow. Now he was so close to the Colonel he could see the scars left from his capture by the Caughna-waga's a few years before when he was only just saved from burning alive by some French officers. It was a broad, tanned face, with a broad high forehead, firm round chin, wide mouth and long straight nose. The long brown hair curled just a trifle. The eyes were large and brown and kindly, and the whole effect of the man was one of strength and serenity and a self-discipline nothing could shake. Suddenly Mark's stomach felt normal again. Here was a man who would listen, and whom he could trust.

"Etty?" the Colonel was saying in a pleasant voice, quite different from the bellow Mark had heard on the ship in the storm. "Of course I remember him. In my company when we fought the French. Hope you've been taking care of yourself, Etty."

"Yes sir," said Simon, with the widest smile Mark had ever seen. "Hope you have too, sir. This is my friend, Mark Woodbridge, from Litchfield. He has a problem he'd like to ask you about, sir."

As the brown eyes glanced at him Mark found himself giving his best salute. "You look young to have problems, or to be here at all, Woodbridge."

"I'm sixteen, sir. And I'm here because I had to get to Cuba."

"His uncle was my friend, sir," Simon put in. "What he's going to tell you won't sound reasonable, but on my word it's the truth."

Putnam smiled. "Long as you aren't telling how many Indians or bears you've killed, I'll believe you, Etty. Sit down. Tell me what it's all about, my boy."

As they sat down, cross-legged, on the ground Mark smiled with relief. There was nothing he couldn't tell this friendly man before him. But he remembered his careful rehearsal, and how he had shortened his story, and started, hesitantly, with the call of Pedro Galvez and Uncle Thad's death.

"That I saw myself," interrupted Simon. "I was there, sir. Show him the button and the dagger, son."

Putnam examined the dagger curiously. "A fine piece," he murmured. "Toledo steel, without a doubt. Go on, Woodbridge."

As briefly as he could, Mark told of finding Uncle Thad's letter and the will, of joining the army, his adventures in New York. Halfway through he was conscious Simon had slid away, but he kept on to his visit to the Casa Hermosa, but left out the night in Havana. Hesitantly he mentioned the rumor that some of the Provincials were to go back on the ships to New York.

Putnam rested his chin on his hand and looked at him searchingly. "As you say, it is a nearly incredible story. And your rumor is right, some of my troops and some of

Colonel Lyman's are returning in a day or so. The orders should come through any time. But your tale . . . show me the will, if you don't mind."

"I can't," faltered Mark. "It was stolen."

"You should have guarded that, as your best proof," Putnam told him sternly.

"We did, sir," chuckled Simon, dropping down beside Mark. "We put it in your strong box."

The Colonel laughed. "Safe, yes. I'll not ask how. But when . . . ? Oh, yes, the other day when the Spanish tried to overrun the camp. Job told me my tent had been entered."

"And that packet was taken then, sir," finished Mark.

With a flourish worthy of a King's officer, Simon pulled a packet from his coat pocket. "The one with your name was taken, but the one with mine was left." He unwrapped the cloth and there lay the folded parchment of the will and the copy of Uncle Thad's letter. With a bow he handed them to a gaping Mark.

"Thought something might happen, even to the Colonel's strong box," said Simon with modest pride, "only from someone who didn't rightly know the Colonel, of course," he added quickly. "So I put a New York Advertiser in the one with your name, Mark, and your things in my name."

"Smart as a fox, as usual, Etty," Putnam approved. "You're forgiven for the use of my strong box. Let me see the will."

Mark put it in the strong hand.

"Even more unintelligible than Greek would be," Putnam murmured, "but it certainly looks authentic. So, young man, this should be certain proof of your story. What do you want of me?"

"Your advice, sir. I . . . I don't see how I can do anything about this inheritance now. I was going to wait until we had the island and then go to the Governor with this will. I thought with English courts and English laws established here I might—what is the word—establish my claim."

"Very sound."

"But if it's true we're being sent back now, there's nothing I can do."

"No. Certainly not now. It will not take long to reduce the city, but longer to establish law and order."

"Could I stay behind, sir, until then?"

Putnam frowned. "I don't see how, Woodbridge. Making an exception. Going against orders. Our British cousins wouldn't understand. Endless explanations, and none of them good. Why, they'd practically raise questions in the House of Commons about it. Very awkward. I'd do it for you and Etty if I could, but I doubt if even Howe or Albemarle themselves could carry it off." He grimaced a little. "The army is pretty strict, as you should know, and while we may do things the easy way on our own territory, we're all under British orders here."

He rose and smiled. "I wish you good luck, young man. Go home, as you have to now. Come down again, say in the winter. In the meantime, if I'm here when the city falls, I'll try to find a good lawyer for you. If I can't, I'll see what I can do in New York. Litchfield, you say? I'll send you word. I'd like to see you have what your uncle left you. It'd be an interesting experiment, what a man from Connecticut could do on this island. But there's nothing you can do now. Patience is a virtue you will have several months to acquire, but you will always find it useful thereafter."

Mark and Simon would have saluted, but Putnam shook hands with each. "Glad you've come through this all right, Etty. Next time we go to fight, come with me again. You, too, Woodbridge, if you aren't settled here. And if you do make it back here and get your Casa, let me know. I'd be curious about how you make out. Good fortune, and good day."

They did salute then, and started back toward the Chorrera.

"It's all very well to say wait and come back," muttered Mark. "I've got to wait. But how'll I ever get back? I haven't a pound to my name."

"You'll think of something," Simon said again. "Now we got to get to those boats."

20

The
Peneranda
Hoard

CAPTAIN Lamson was lounging beside their hut when they returned. "Sit down," he ordered harshly. "I want to talk with you."

Mark stepped back. "I don't have to . . ." he began.

Simon nudged him. "Go ahead. He's a captain now, but he won't be next time we meet."

Lamson sat down himself out of arm's length, his pale eyes flickering from one to another. "You diddled me for fair," he began, with an air of open frankness. "I wanted to congratulate you."

"Like the devil congratulated the preacher," said Simon. "Go on."

Lamson looked Simon up and down. "That was your idea, Etty, putting the newspaper in that packet. I won't forget it." He turned back to Mark. "Were you really in Havana two nights ago, or was that a gammon of Peneranda's?"

Mark hesitated.

"Give me that paper," Lamson rapped out like an order. "Hand it over."

Before he thought Mark's hand moved a little upward towards his belt.

"So you were there, and you do have it," the harsh voice was satisfied. "Don't know where you got it, nor does Peneranda, but I wouldn't be in your shoes when he catches up with you."

"How'd you know where to look for the other papers, yourself, Captain?" Simon broke in smoothly.

Lamson looked pleased. "Figured it out," he said complacently. "You couldn't keep the will around you. But you'd bring it with you. Found out most officers don't have a strong box, but colonels do. And when I saw Putnam's orderly I knew he was a friend of Etty's, just by his looks. Simple. And then you did me out of a thousand pounds."

"You'd never have gotten anything out of Peneranda," said Mark.

The Captain smiled unpleasantly. "Don't be too sure of that, me lad. But now I want that paper. He said it was blank, but there must be something on it. He's fair frothing at the mouth about it, though he tries to hide that. Acts nonchalant. Says he has ways, and that you'll never get the Hoard. For the last time, hand over that paper and I'll go after the Hoard myself and split what I find. I offered that before and I offer it again. All I want is enough to live well. There'll be plenty for us both, by what he says."

Mark shook his head. All three rose as though pulled by strings. The pale eyes slitted. "Hand it over. Or I'll go to your Captain for an order."

"Wouldn't advise that," drawled Simon. "Olcott's a good friend. And we got a lot of other friends around here, too." He nodded down the company street. "You wouldn't get far trying to force anything, mister."

A muscle in Lamson's cheek twitched a moment. "All right, for now," he said softly. "I can wait." He strode down the street.

Two hours later Captain Olcott read the orders to the cheering men. His company and one from Rhode Island and two from the Chorrera camp were to return to New York and be disbanded. They must be prepared to move out the next day, though there might be a day's delay after that.

"Got nothing to prepare." Nat gestured widely towards the huts, the trees, the hard earth. "Only got myself, and that's been ready since we landed."

"Will we share the prize money when the army takes the city?" asked someone.

"No one's told me that," Olcott answered sourly. "But it's likely."

"It'll be prize enough to get out of this stinking place, sir," called Nat. And that seemed to be the general opinion.

"So it's true." Mark felt as if the end of the world was coming. "And I'll never be able to get back here." He thought of the Casa Hermosa, which could be made beautiful again, and of the chest full of jewels. Jewels! Jewels meant money, and money would pay for a passage back when the island was safely under English rule. If he had the Peneranda Hoard he could come back, claim all the inheritance, hire lawyers, from England if need be—why—do anything! He buffeted Simon on the shoulder. "The chest! We're going for it tonight."

"Had a hunch you'd think of that, after a bit," allowed Simon seriously. "Worth a try. But might be a job finding that spot. Couldn't wait another night?"

"I'll send Angelo for Roberto. He'll guide us. We can't wait. If we did—we'd sail tomorrow."

Simon rubbed the back of his head. "All right. It's up to you to say. I'd kinda like to wait, though, see what happens."

"Too much could happen," Mark pointed out, "particularly with men at the Casa now. They won't know where to go, but they'll be searching."

"Then we better take Tom Davidson with us," Simon said decisively. "We'll need another hand, and he's a good lad in a fight."

It was just before moonrise that the three met Roberto and Angelo at the crossroads near the Casa. Mark had told Angelo he needed Roberto to help him find a certain place. Now he told more, of the shore of the bay and the dry river.

Roberto nodded. "*Si*, I know the place, *Señor*."

"And I," shrilled Angelo. "I know, too."

"No," Mark told him sternly. "You can't come, Angelo. You might get hurt, or something."

"Then I go elsewhere," said Angelo quickly, in a small voice. "As I was told . . . *Hola!* There is that Tomás, who has been following us. I will scare him away."

Simon clamped a hand on Angelo's shoulder. "I'll scare him." He nodded toward a small figure that was edging closer. "You get going, Angelo."

It was impossible to see if the small figure who, as Simon advanced, took to his heels toward the Casa was Tomás or not.

When the walls of the Casa Hermosa were left behind the thread of a path plunged into woods as thick as those of the Cavannas. It took a half hour to reach the bay, wide and empty and glimmering palely in the moonlight. The dry river was another ten minutes from the edge of the shore. By now the moon had reached the treetops. Mark looked at it and stumbled on a rock. Surely this was a different moon from the friendly yellow face he knew at home. This was somehow larger and whiter and frightening. Something dreadful was going to happen beneath it.

"Good to stretch the legs again," Tom Davidson said behind him, and dispelled his mood.

At the first heap of boulders Roberto stopped. "I go no farther," he whispered, his hands twisting in front of him. "I am afraid. I no want know more, see more. You find way back?"

"Sure, sonny," Simon assured him heartily, patting his shoulder. "You've done fine. Thank you."

Roberto looked at Mark timidly. "You no angry, *Señor?* I no want get caught."

"I'm not angry," Mark told him. "I understand. Thank you."

With a timid, grateful smile, Roberto slipped into the woods.

The moonlight on the irregular jumble of rocks gave an effect of a broad, jagged road, half silver, half black, in the light and shadow, running up the low hill between the trees, its edges dappled by the gentle moving branches above.

"We won't try to go up that mess," said Simon. "Take us an hour to climb over those boulders. We'll go along this bank, like we were told, just above the edge there and watch for those three rocks."

More than once shadows deceived them, but five minutes later the three rocks making the tent stood out clearly. There was a little space at the base of the triangle, and

Mark wondered why this had not been chosen for the hiding place, and then decided it was too obvious, while the tent formation made an unmovable landmark. They passed the rocks and slid down the bank. Yes, just below where dirt and roots met boulders, was a flat stone, half in light, half in shadow. Mark caught his breath. Somehow he had not quite believed it until now. He shivered. It was very quiet in the woods; not even a night bird cheeped.

"That'll take some digging." Simon rubbed the back of his head thoughtfully. "Wish we had a crowbar."

"I fell over a good hard log we might use," offered Tom. "I'll get it while you dig."

They had moved the smaller rocks from around the flat one by the time Tom returned with a heavy branch. Moving another rock, Mark found a hollow beneath the slab. The branch fitted into the hole. Tom leaned his weight on the end, and slowly, slowly the flat rock lifted. Tom grunted, rested, and thrust the branch in farther. "Catch the rock this time. I think we've got it. Isn't as heavy as it looks."

Kneeling on either side, Mark and Simon caught the rock with both hands as it was lifted, caught it, and eased it upright to stand on end in the cavity. All three knelt beside the hollow. An iron chest, perhaps two feet long, could be clearly seen.

"What's that?" asked Tom.

"What we came for," Mark mumbled. Suppose it was empty?

The handles at each end of the chest were needed, for the hole was deep and it was hard to get a good grip. Twice it slipped, and Mark nearly cried out. Then at last it was on the ground in the moonlight.

"Open it, Mark," Simon said quietly. "It's yours."

Suppose it's locked, thought Mark. His fingers trembled as he knelt in front of the chest and fumbled at the hasps. They lifted, and with a creak the lid stood open.

All three let out a gasp. The chest was filled with molten fire; red, white, blue, green, flashed in a myriad of sparkling stars, as if the whole heaven and the sun and stars together had been poured within.

"Jiminy," was all Tom could say. "What's that?"

"The Peneranda Hoard," Simon answered, "and I must say it's prettier than anything I've seen."

"Is it real?"

"Uncle Thad said so," whispered Mark. "But . . . but I never thought it would be like this. He was aghast. He'd heard the phrase "wealth of the Indies." This is what it must mean.

Lying on top of the glittering mass was a black leather bag. That was Uncle Thad's. Mark reached a shaking hand, felt the hardness of stones inside, and slid it into his trouser pocket. That was surely his, but this other . . . no one man would know what to do with all that. "Take some," he said hoarsely. "Take some. I . . . I don't know what to do."

Simon hesitated. "It's not right, somehow, but I've always been partial to the looks of icicles." His hand fumbled a minute and picked up a star that glowed and glittered coldly.

"Still don't believe it's real," breathed Tom. "But if you say so, I'm partial to red." His hand closed slowly over a deeply gleaming stone.

Mark could only look. He had never seen anything so

214

beautiful. No wonder Uncle Thad and Don Diego had kept the stones for the pleasure of looking at them.

"Come on," Simon broke the silence brusquely. "We still got to get this back to camp. And we better get going."

Reluctantly Mark closed and fastened the chest. "You're right." His hands were still shaking. Could jewels make anyone shake, or was he just weak-minded?

It was a hard, panting job to get the chest up to the top of the bank. Pushing, shoving, hauling, propelled by a strange new urgency, they stumbled hurriedly toward the shore as fast as the narrow path and deceptive shadows permitted. At the edge of the bay, where the tumble of rocks halted abruptly in flat sand, they set it down to rest. Far ahead bay and sea and sky melted together into a blue mist. In front the ripples lapped the white shore in broken lines of gold. Behind loomed the dark of bushes and trees pressing down to the beach. The forest was no longer quiet but filled with little rustlings.

"We better get moving," urged Simon, in an uneasy voice. "It's a long trip back."

"We'll get there." Mark tried to sound confident. "But I haven't figured out what to do with it when we do."

On the bank behind them a twig snapped. "Make for the rocks," ordered Simon sharply. "Someone's coming."

"We are not only coming, we are here," purred the detestable voice of Pedro Peneranda. "And you, boy, will not have to worry what to do with the contents of the chest."

From the woods seeped a group of white-clad men. In front of them strode Peneranda, smiling like a satisfied cat. "Don't move," he cracked, as Simon made a gesture toward his belt. "Gaspar, see if they have weapons."

Grinning widely the squat foreman moved toward Simon. Mark looked around. There must have been fifteen men. Some held axes, others pikes, some scythes and a few muskets. There was no place to run: the circle was complete. Gaspar plucked the pistol from Simon, sneered when he found nothing on Tom, and gaped in surprise as he pulled the silver dagger from Mark's belt. He cast a frightened glance at Peneranda and held it out to him.

"Ah, yes. This is returned, for the last time." The man took it in his right hand, balancing it delicately. He looked at Mark with eyes shining yet opaque in the moonlight. Mark looked back steadily, though his stomach knotted. Those eyes said there would be no mistake, and no mercy, this time. But the gaze shifted to the chest.

"So you did find the Peneranda Hoard. I was sure you would discover it, for me. When Tomás reported you were going through the wood toward the bay I knew we had only to follow. It seems we arrived just in time."

"Are you not going to make sure it is the Hoard, *Señor?*" asked Gaspar obsequiously.

"In front of this scum?" He nodded toward the narrowing circle of men. "You are mad. They will carry it to the Casa. And bring these three."

"Not just yet," rang out another voice. All heads turned. On the beach, just beyond the circle of men, stood Captain Lamson. His uniform was torn and there were red marks on his wrists, but he held a pistol steadily in each hand.

"Thought you'd got rid of me, eh Peneranda? But I never drank your poisoned wine. You were too pleased with yourself to notice. And when your men tied me they were careless." His voice sharpened. "Tell your men not to throw any knives. I'll shoot you before any reach me."

Peneranda said something, and two arms lowered.

"Come on, Gaspar," called Lamson, his voice tight and excited. "Open that chest. Let's be sure we've got the jewels at last."

Gaspar hurried to the chest, undid the clasps and threw back the lid. A sound like a sigh of wind, that rose to a near shriek, came from the dark-faced men as the moonlight poured into the glittering mass. Mark jerked his eyes away and looked at Peneranda. The man's teeth were bared in a wolfish grin, his whole face pointed, avid, exulting. Lamson moved nearer and gave a sound like a sob.

"That's it, all right," he said unsteadily. "Close it, Gaspar."

"You fool," snarled Peneranda. "Do you think you will get one diamond, now they have seen—that?"

"Oh, yes, for I will promise them shares, which is more than you have done."

"You would give them—that?" Peneranda's voice was a rasping cry. "You . . ." Silver dagger upraised he rushed toward Lamson. One pistol shot rang out. The black-clad figure swayed to one side.

Lamson shifted his remaining pistol to his right hand. "Stop, you fool."

Lamson ducked and fired, and Peneranda was on him. The silver dagger flashed once. The black figure poised like a huge bat over the fallen man, straightened, and wiped the dagger on the blue coat. A slight smile on the thin lips, he strolled back to the circle.

"We might as well finish it all here and now." Thoughtfully he looked at the three soldiers. "I had thought to take you to the Casa, but I should not indulge myself."

Mark turned to Simon despairingly. With fifteen men around them what could anyone do?

Simon's head was cocked to one side and he was looking curiously at Peneranda. "You may not get it all back, yourself," he said softly, and pointed.

One of the peons had snaked forward on his stomach until his hand had reached the open chest. Oblivious of all around him, like a brown crab his hand was reaching up and inward.

"*Bestia*," hissed Peneranda. He seized an axe from the peon beside him. Half-crouching, he stepped towards the chest. The brown fingers had closed on a glowing diamond. Peneranda whirled the axe and struck the man's shoulder with the flat of the blade, knocking him to the sand. At a harsh order two other men moved sullenly to the prone figure, jerked it upright and stood holding the arms. The man drooped and sagged farther and cried out as Peneranda gave another order.

"Aaaaah," sighed the circle of men.

"A lesson for all." Peneranda swung in a circle to face them. "The man will hang when we return to the Casa and there is more time." He dropped the axe on the sand and stared at Mark. "That is *my* brand of Peneranda justice. Gaspar, close and fasten the chest."

Once more Peneranda, his teeth bared in an evil smile, glanced around the circle, ending with Simon. Slowly he drew the silver dagger from his pocket. "It would be better to kill you one by one, now," he said casually. "It would drive home my lesson of what I do to thieves. There is time." He glanced back at Mark. "You will see your friends die."

As Mark faced him terror swept over him again. His

heart was thumping and his throat was tight. He was powerless in the concentrated venom of that narrow murderous face. And then, from somewhere deep inside him, he knew he could not let himself be afraid of such a man. He could not let Simon be killed on his account. He blinked once, to clear his sight, threw his weight forward on his toes and launched himself at the black figure. His right fist aimed for the pointed chin, and grazed it. His left fist hit the shoulder so hard Peneranda spun sideways. Mark's arms were seized from behind in the mighty grip of Gaspar, as his feet were jerked out from under him.

"Good try," called Simon.

Mark twisted his head. Simon and Tom, back to back, faced a tight ring. Simon's head was cocked on one side as though listening.

Gaspar pulled Mark up to face Peneranda. The silver dagger gleamed in the white hand. Peneranda slid one foot forward, leaned a little, and flicked Mark's cheek with the point. As Mark jerked his head back he felt the knife slide downward.

Mark made himself straighten and look squarely at the triumphant face.

21

The Silver Dagger

"*Hola!*" rang out Simon's shout behind him. "*Ayuda! Aqui!*"

A flood of men poured out of the woods, down the bank, from behind the tumbled rocks. Brown faces intent, expressionless, their silence was more terrifying than any shouting would have been.

Peneranda, oblivious, his eyes fastened on Mark's, stepped forward again. He raised the dagger. A blow descended on his arm. The dagger fell to the sand. In spite of himself Mark sagged. He felt the man clasping his legs loosen his hold.

"Beltran!" rumbled Gaspar.

Beside Peneranda stood a broad-shouldered stalwart figure in loose white shirt and trousers, a musket held easily in front of him. The moonlight showed a broad calm face with high cheek bones, large eyes and a strong chin. One low word to Gaspar and Mark was freed. He would have liked to let his knees buckle, but he made them straighten and threw back his shoulders. He could feel the blood running down his cheek.

The man looked at him searchingly a minute, then suddenly smiled. "*Señor* Mark, it must be," he said slowly in careful English.

Mark found he could march forward and hold out his hand. "I am truly glad to see you, Beltran," he managed.

Beltran's smile was kind. "I feared I would not get here when it was necessary. It makes me happy I did."

Mark let out a long gust of breath. Peneranda was held by two men, his face again a mask. Behind him, each of his men was held firmly by two of the newcomers. There were three encircling Gaspar. Mark smiled shakily. "It makes me happy, too."

"Can't say how glad I am to see you," said Simon as he moved up beside Mark. Tom could only give a half salute as he wiped his forehead. "Nearest I ever hope to come to being killed," he muttered.

"And I, too, am happy to see you." Gaspar inserted his oily voice feverishly between them. "I would have had a hard time protecting the young *Señor* from that man. And these other men, they are beasts, they would have killed all."

"Be silent, you fool," commanded Peneranda lazily, and Gaspar cringed back. Peneranda half turned toward Beltran. "So the escaped slave returns?" he sneered. "And with an armed band. That is insurrection, and punishable by death." On the sand, the silver dagger shone as brightly as a jewel.

"He's not a slave," Mark cried hotly. "Don Diego freed him long ago."

"But I saw to it that the law did not recognize many of Don Diego's actions. This Beltran was my slave, until he escaped."

"Yes." Beltran gave him a long, level look. "And I have not forgotten, nor have my men, the dungeons of the Casa and the things you and Gaspar and others did to us."

"Only under orders," whined Gaspar. "I was as much a slave . . ." One of the men struck him across the mouth.

Peneranda moved his shoulders as though he would have shrugged. "Enough of that. It is forgotten. I, also, will forget. Take your men, and those three, back to the hills, Beltran. I will say nothing to the authorities of this exploit. On the honor of a Peneranda."

Beltran's face went bleak. "You are the last of the Peneranda, and yet you have no honor. Don Diego, God rest his soul, was always ashamed of you. And he knew not the depth of your—your infamy."

Peneranda's face contorted. "You dare speak thus?"

"I dare. And well you know that when we return to the hills you would be powerless against us. The question is— what to do with you." He raised his voice. "*Compañeros!*" he called. "*Que haceriamos?*"

Like a coming storm a low mutter swept around the circle. The word sounded like "*Muerte.*"

"That means kill," murmured Simon.

"Yes," agreed Beltran somberly. "They vote to kill. Not one is here who has not been suffering at his orders."

"You would not dare," Peneranda sneered.

"*Joya!*" A protesting cry came from one figure. "*Joya!*" It was the man who had reached for the diamond. He had shaken free of his guards and was pointing to the chest. The circle closed inward.

"You have found it, then," observed Beltran. "I am glad."

"They have found only what is mine." Peneranda raised

his voice a little and spoke icily, commandingly in Spanish.

"He's telling them to kill Gaspar," translated Simon in a low voice. "That Gaspar's the one who's been doing the killing."

A growl of assent followed.

Gaspar shrieked and threw off the men who had been holding his arms. He stooped, picked up the axe from the sand, and swung it around him. The nearest men shrank back. Peneranda stood, expressionless, well out of range of the circling weapon. The man condemned to hang was crawling toward him.

The beach was filled with clamor. Gaspar's shouts rose above the others, and ever the axe head swung around him.

"Why don't you shoot?" Simon asked softly as they stepped back a little.

"Because, *Señor*, we have no bullets," Beltran answered wryly. "It will all end as fate wills."

Though fascinated by the silver streak made by the circling axe head, Mark noticed that Peneranda had stepped yet farther away and was nearing the single row of Beltran's men, who had eyes only for Gaspar. He glanced at Beltran, and saw he was also watching.

"*Hola!* Gaspar!" Beltran shouted. "Don Pedro . . ."

Gaspar whirled. Peneranda made a dash between two of the men and was thrust back by two solid arms. The axe was raised. Peneranda twisted sideways and backwards as the axe handle twisted in Gaspar's hands. The back of the axe struck his shoulder. It was enough to knock him to one knee. Beside him a man rose from a crouch. Like a falling star the dagger descended into the black back.

Gaspar rushed forward. Pulling out the dagger, the man

turned to meet him. Axe upraised Gaspar tripped over the legs of Peneranda and fell forward on the upthrust dagger. A sigh, part horror part relief, escaped from the men.

Mark would have liked to cover his eyes. He appealed silently to Simon, who nodded understandingly.

"We're going to walk down the beach a piece and wait for you," he said to Beltran, who nodded in turn. "*Si, Señor*. That is better."

Holding himself very straight and trying not to run, Mark managed to reach the shadow of a clump of bushes at the edge of the bank. Simon and Tom moved slowly ahead. When he was himself again he hurried through the moonlight to join them, where they sat on the white sand.

Tom's face was white and he was shaking his head. "Never saw anything like it," he was saying over and over.

"And you likely won't again, as the farmer said of the two-headed calf," Simon broke in briskly. "Best thing that could have happened all around."

"I . . . I suppose so." Mark found his voice uncertain. "But, all at once . . ."

"Peneranda and Gaspar had it coming to them, by all accounts and as we saw for ourselves," Simon pointed out. "Lamson was asking for trouble when he tangled with Peneranda. No use thinking about it more." He tapped Mark on the shoulder. "Young fellow, have you thought what you're going to do with that chest of jewels?"

"Take it back to the camp, I suppose," Mark answered hesitantly. "Then home on the ship."

"Have you thought how you're going to keep it a secret, get it on the ship, keep it a secret on the ship? Even if you rope it, how many jewels do you suppose will be left by the time you get to New York?"

Mark rubbed his cheek and looked wonderingly at the red on his fingers. "No," he faltered. "I . . . I haven't had time to think."

"Well, you better start thinking fast. Here comes Beltran."

Still holding his useless musket Beltran squatted down before them. "I regret, *Señores,* that you have witnessed this . . . this thing. Be assured none of my men will ever speak of it."

"What are you going to do with the dead ones?" Tom gestured toward the distant group.

"The three will disappear and never be found. Do not concern yourself." He glanced at Mark. "What is your wish about the chest, *Señor* Mark?"

"I . . . I don't know." Mark's head was aching. But there was one thing he wanted to know. "How did you happen to come just now, and save us? I . . . I thank you again."

Beltran smiled gently. "But no thanks are due me from the nephew of *Señor* T'ad. And I came because of both Angelo and Roberto. When each left you he ran to my camp."

"But they said you were far away in the mountains with outlaws."

"That has been true. But Mama Hanno sent me word you were here, you would need me. So I and some of my men moved down to be, what you say, at hand."

"But how did Mama Hanno know I'd need you?"

"I told her," Simon admitted. "Had a hunch she knew how to get word to Beltran. After your trip to Havana I knew we'd be in trouble. When you're outnumbered it makes sense to get help."

Mark shook his head. "You've all been smarter than I was."

"Not smarter," Simon said gently. "Just older. More used to thinking ahead."

"What about that silver knife?" Tom asked. "Where's it now?"

"The thirsty dagger has gone where it will thirst no more."

"Who will get the Peneranda lands now?" Simon broke in.

"Who knows? A distant cousin who lives in Spain, it is my belief."

"Hope he'll be a good master, but likely not. Now, Mark, what about the chest?"

Mark looked across the calm bay to the distant dark line of the opposite shore. "You're right," he began awkwardly. "That's more of you thinking when I didn't. Even with some of the men to help we'd have a hard time getting it back to camp. And even if we asked the Captain to take care of it, it wouldn't be a secret long. And I don't know what I'd do with all those jewels. Peneranda and Lamson, they talked of travel, horses, castles, but that would be all so strange to me. Uncle Thad'd have known how to use such money the right way. But I can't see myself just doing nothing."

He looked away from the bay to the three faces, Simon's wise and sympathetic, Tom open-mouthed, Beltran's friendly but noncommittal.

"Besides," he went on, "it doesn't really seem right to take it all away from here. All those jewels weren't Uncle Thad's. They were Don Diego's. Oh, I know Don Diego left them to Uncle Thad, but that's not me. I think they ought to stay here and be used."

He turned to Beltran. "I didn't know how your people lived until I got here. I didn't know how the Spanish treated you, until I saw Roberto being beaten, until Serafina was killed because of her cow, until I saw how people lived in that village. Couldn't the jewels be turned into money to help the people?"

"What do you suggest, *Señor?*" Beltran asked carefully. "Here it would be difficult to make our lot easier even by one cow for which a man could not explain."

Mark rubbed his forehead tiredly. "Well, isn't there some other place you could go? Look. We're going to take Havana soon, and everything's going to be in a mess on this island for a long time after that. Couldn't you and your men and your families, and perhaps some others, slip away somewhere?"

Beltran's face almost lit up from inside. He looked happy, eager, then it became calm again. "But yes, *Señor.* That is possible. The thought has come to me in the past. Never had it seemed possible."

"But you helped bury that chest in the first place, didn't you?" asked Simon curiously. "You could have taken whatever you wanted."

The man opposite stiffened. "It was not mine to take, *Señor.* It belonged to *Señor* T'ad. But now, it is different." He began to speak more quickly. "I have seen the English are more kind to people than the Spanish. Myself I have made a trip to Jamaica. There we could go, a few at a time, you understand. I could go first and buy some land, oh, far away from cities. On our own land we would do well. I have friends in the city. I could sell a jewel at a time, enough for some land, a cow, some pigs. Or, if not Jamaica, there are other islands. . . ." He looked excited again. "It might be, *Señor*."

Mark rubbed his head again. The moonlight on the moving water was making his eyes ache. "Isn't that what both Don Diego and *Señor* Thad would wish?" he asked. "From Uncle Thad's letter it sounded as if Don Diego took good care of his people, when it was suggested to him. And that last note said to give you some of the jewels, and to use the rest wisely. Isn't that what Uncle Thad would like to see done?"

"For me it is not to say, *Señor*—but if it is your wish. . . . Yet it is not right that of it all the nephew of *Señor* T'ad should not have his share."

"I couldn't take any with me on the ship," Mark said again.

"There's always Old Put," drawled Simon. "Job's not likely to let anyone near Put's dispatch box again. And after I talk with him a bit he'll be offering himself to carry north anything I give him 'cause he lost us those papers once."

Mark remembered Job's shrewd cold gray eye and the sturdy strength of the General. "Yes," he admitted, "that'd be safe."

"And you might take a speck of time to look at it all from Thad's side," Simon went on carefully. "He and the Don'd gone to a heap of trouble to put the Hoard away safe for Thad. And no strings on it at all as to what Thad did with it. And Thad did his best to make sure you got it, whether he was along or not."

Beltran nodded slowly. "That is right, *Señor*."

"Well, you aren't likely ever to get the Casa and the other things in the will. But you got that." He gestured toward the rocks. "There's things you could do for your people, too, you know. You could get Debby and Elisha a real good farm. You got your mind set on college. Can't go there for free. Later, you might hanker for a farm of your own. Or a business. And then there's Thad's friends out to the Todman place. They could do with a real good house to live in that didn't have cracks so wide in the walls a jay bird could walk through. They'd take to real food and clothes, too. Or a school house, now. Thad believed in schooling. There's a mort of useful things could be done with money in your own town for your own people."

"It's the truth," Tom said soberly.

"And this is but honorable and right," Beltran began earnestly. "In the chest is much jewels. In my lifetime I could not spend it all for my people. For others it should be used also."

Mark saw the gray walls of the Todman house, the sagging barn. His father's farm had never really had good crops. The one-room schoolhouse in town was too small to hold all the children. Yes, there were things he could do with the money that Uncle Thad would approve. A good place for Debby, too. He could not see beyond college for himself, but perhaps someday he could go to England and see Edward. Simon, he should have a chance to do whatever he wished. "All right," he exclaimed, "let's divide it. Half for Don Diego's people, half for Uncle Thad's."

"What you going to carry it back to camp in?" Tom asked, as they walked back. "Can't go lugging that chest around."

"The chest, with our share, I will again bury," Beltran told them. "For you, for now, we will take a shirt to be a bag."

The dead men had already vanished from the sand. Beltran's band had melted again into the lights and shadows of the woods, taking Don Pedro's people with them. Beltran stepped into the darkness and returned with a shirt he quickly knotted into a sizeable sack. The moon again struck fire from the chest, but now the jewels were more than jewels, they were food and houses and land, and somehow Mark did not feel so overcome by their beauty. The chest was upturned and they knelt by the glittering heap.

"If you trust me, *Señor*, I will divide?" Beltran asked tentatively. "I know something of these from Don Diego. I will be fair."

"Of course I trust you," Mark assured him warmly. "Uncle Thad did."

Beltran's smile was wide and slow, and then his brown hands moved swiftly, dividing diamonds, rubies, sapphires, emeralds, jeweled boxes and buckles, a small pile of gold coins. Mark found himself watching the man and not the jewels. The wide bronze face, with a square forehead, high cheekbones and square chin showed Indian blood, and perhaps Spanish as well. He realized he had spoken without thought, except of his uncle's trust, when he offered half the jewels to Beltran, but now he was sure he was right. This man would act calmly and carefully and wisely.

When the two piles were even they sat back on their heels.

"We'd look like northern lights ourselves if we went into camp decked out in that," Simon chuckled.

Tom snorted at the picture. "And we wouldn't look like that long."

Mark laughed. Suddenly he felt lighter, gayer, as though a dark cloud was lifted from around him. "But it would be a treat to see the Captain's face."

Beltran called over his shoulder, then faced them again. "In the shirt we can carry to the Casa. In the kitchen are small chests once for coffee or spices for the cook. In one of those we can put this."

As they shoveled the sparkling mound onto the cloth Mark asked, "Do you happen to know an outlaw leader who calls himself El Gallo?"

Beltran cocked his head to one side. "*Si, Señor.* So it was you who found for El Gallo the fine new body of men and the ten muskets. It was cleverly done."

Mark hoped no one could see his blush. No one had ever called him clever before. "It was the only thing I could think of," he said quickly. "But I hope no one was hurt."

"A few cracked heads, which is nothing," Beltran smiled. "And the new men now are happy that they do not need to go and fight the English."

"And the officer?"

"He was a problem." Mark could see how anguished that long sallow face would look at being a problem himself. "But the next day he was led to near Guanamacoa and released. There is such confusion he will come to no harm."

"What will happen to El Gallo?"

"Under the English they will, what is it, scatter, perhaps to the forests, or to other parts of the island, for a new life. Had I known you were seeking the portrait at Casa Alta the trip you made I could have saved you."

"Wouldn't have missed it," Mark assured him solemnly. Then, remembering, he began to laugh until he rolled sideways to the sand. "Wish I had time to tell you," he gasped. "Ask Georgie about our adventures, but don't believe everything." He sat up. "Yes, Beltran. At Casa Alta you will now find one who calls himself Georgie Smith. He says he comes from Jamaica, which I believe, and perhaps some of the other things he said. But he may be able to help you. He knows something of business, of Jamaica and Spanish Town. He says he does not betray his own side. But don't trust him with ha'pence, and remember he likes an easy life and good food, which is very important to his health."

"Then through his stomach I will control him. I will seek him. And I do not trust many people, *Señor* Mark."

When the improvised sack was filled, they helped Beltran return the other half of the glowing heap to the chest, and return it to its hiding place.

"One other I trust I will tell of this place. I will come and take of it as I need. But it will take years to do all that I can already see ahead, for I must move slowly so there will be no questions. And always there will be much more here than I can use. *Señor* Mark, if you have need, or wish, and return, what is here is yours."

The four took turns carrying the heavy sack, slung on a stick across their shoulders. The moon was down in the west now, the light milky pale, the palm trees stiff feathery tufts. In the kitchen at the Casa a small solid chest was already washed and lined with moss. The sack was emptied into the chest and moss added to hold all in place. At the last minute Mark remembered Uncle Thad's own small sack and the packet with the will and dropped them on the top.

From the forge Beltran brought an iron chain and a crow-bar to open and close links in place of a lock.

"José and Antonio will carry it to the big mahogany tree by your camp and guard it until you wish to take it away. It is better I should return with the others."

Beyond the rusty gates they halted. Mark held out his hand.

"Thank you, Beltran, for . . . for everything . . . for guarding the jewels, and for taking care of your people, and for coming tonight when we needed you, and for being Uncle Thad's friend, and mine. And good luck."

His hand was clasped firmly in the two broad ones. "But my thanks are to you, Señor Mark, and for your trust. I will do my best, as Señor T'ad and Don Diego and you would wish for my people. I thank you for them. Go with God, and our blessings will be with you always."

22

Northward
Bound

THE company was routed out early, for word had come they would board ship that afternoon.

"What are you going to do about that chest?" asked Simon, as he worked on his boots. "We can't leave it by the mahogany tree very long."

"I was wondering about it when I went to sleep last night," Mark said slowly. In the sunlight all that had happened in the shimmer of moonlight seemed far away and unreal. But Simon's words made it real. "I think I know now. The one person I trust is Edward Manning. He'll know how to get it safely to New York. I'm going to see him now."

"An English officer'll keep his word, if he's a gentleman," Simon agreed. "Young Manning's a knowledgeable lad. But there's always Old Put . . ."

"No. We'd never be able to get that chest into a boat and down to Chorrera without the whole army knowing about it. And he's too busy a man to be bothered now. Edward will know what to do."

He was finishing mess when Mark arrived. "So early!"

he exclaimed. "And what happened to your face? What's the matter?"

"We're leaving, and I need your help. There's not much time. Where can we talk?"

As they stood on the rocks above the shore and watched the longboats of the ships scurry back and forth across the water, Mark sketched his tale.

"Wish I'd been with you," Edward said wistfully. "I'd have liked to see it all. But I know there wasn't time to get me . . ."

At the problem of the chest Edward's eyes lightened. "Of course I'll help. And I can. My cousin, John Chisholm, the lieutenant in the 56th, has the honor of carrying the dispatches telling of the fall of La Punta this morning." There was pride in the clear voice. "He goes on a fast frigate to New York this afternoon. He's a decent chap. He'll take your chest, and no one will dare touch it if it's in his cabin."

They found Lieutenant Chisholm in his tent watching his orderly pack his dress uniform. "I've heard of you from Edward," he told Mark gaily. "He maintains that if all colonials are like you the colonies must be a good place to live."

Mark smiled across at Edward. "Cornet Manning has given me a high opinion of the English, sir."

Chisholm looked from one to the other. "What can I do for you two? I'm rather pressed for time . . ."

"It's very important," burst out Edward, "and only you, John, can help. May we talk to you, please?"

When the orderly had left Mark told of the chest, something he had inherited, which he could not take on a crowded transport. Chisholm looked at him curiously. "You both look as serious as if a king's ransom was involved," he remarked banteringly. "Glad to take the chest, whatever it holds, for you, Woodbridge. Get it here as soon as you can, and I'll have my man burn my name on it. I'll see myself it's put in my cabin."

"Thank you, sir." That seemed inadequate, but it was the best he could do. "And where can I get it? And . . . you promise?" he asked hesitantly.

Chisholm flashed an understanding smile. "It must indeed be important to you. But I promise, on my honor as an officer and a gentleman, Woodbridge, that I will deliver your chest, unopened, to Walter Livingstone, the merchant who lives on Hanover Square. And I promise he will hold it for you until you yourself call for it."

Mark let out his breath. "Thank you, once more, sir, for everything."

"I'll be staying with Livingstone until the ship leaves for England, so that is easy. Some day I hope to hear the story from Edward." His friendly laugh made him seem less the formidable young officer. "And good luck, Woodbridge."

"I'll wait here for you," Edward said outside the tent. "Bring the chest and I'll watch it myself. I'll make sure John takes it in his own boat, too."

José and Antonio were sitting beneath the mahogany tree, a mound of branches beside them. They rose respectfully as Mark approached and uncovered the chest, which rested on some planks. Mark realized it would look odd at any other time to be going through the British camp with two peons behind him, but he hoped that the bustle and confusion of the day and the departing Provincials would make anything seem reasonable. The two men picked up the planks and followed him obediently. Fascinated and awed by the spectacle of military might around them, they stumbled and swerved through the British camp to Chisholm's tent, where Edward was waiting. Mark had only a shilling left in his belt, and wished it were more, but the two looked as pleased as though it were a diamond. Muttering "*Con Dios*," they moved away slowly, their heads swiveling from side to side at the marvels around them.

Edward whistled at the size of the chain that encircled the chest. "That'll keep it safe, all right. It'd take a forge to get it off. I'll see to everything now."

"Will you be coming to New York yourself?" Mark asked.

"Depends on where the regiment's sent next," Edward answered soberly. "But it might happen."

"Would you come and visit me? Litchfield would always reach me. There're a lot of things we could do."

"I'd like to come. I will, first chance. And you, you'll be traveling. You must come and see me in England. Frampton Manor, Surrey, will reach me. I'll send you word where we're ordered."

They looked at each other solemnly. "I'm glad to have an English friend," Mark said hesitantly. "And thanks for all your help."

Edward looked extra solemn. "I'm glad we're friends. I'll always remember the things we've done together."

Mark had a sudden picture of Edward taking off the officers on the sun-baked parapet of Fort Coximar. He began to laugh. "I hope you'll have some more officers to mimic next time."

Edward glanced around hastily. "Ssssh. Don't let anyone

hear you." His quick grin belonged to that other Edward. "Wherever we go, I'm sure I'll have more for you. And I promise no more ladders."

There was so much to say, too much to say anything more. The two shook hands quickly, nodded, and Mark hurried away.

Back at camp half the stores and gear were already moved down to the shore. Olcott cocked an eyebrow when Mark passed, but said nothing. Angelo was waiting by the hut. For the first time Mark noticed that the boy looked heavier and stronger than on that first afternoon. Meager as the rations had been, they had at least helped Angelo, for a while.

Simon poked his head out of the hut like an owl from a hole. "All set? Good. Angelo has a message."

"Mama Hanno send me tell you come say *adios,* you and *El Señor* Etty," Angelo announced, wide-eyed and solemn. "Come now?"

At Mark's doubtful look Simon shrugged. "No one will know the difference but Olcott and he won't care if we're gone an hour. We owe it to her for likely her water saved a lot of us. And she took good care of me. Come along now."

Angelo was so subdued as he trotted beside the path that Mark asked him what was the matter.

"Me sad, *muy lastimoso,* for you, *El Señor,* all men leave," came in a small voice.

"Well, we'll miss you, too," Mark told him awkwardly. "Why, we couldn't have gotten along at all without you."

The big brown eyes brightened. "*Gracias.* That makes me more happy." He looked around and dropped his voice.

"Roberto already go on with Beltran. I go follow, now."

At the crossroads he held out his hand. *"Adios, Señor* Etty, *Señor* Mark. *Me orgulloso* to have helped, to be your *amigo."* There was a touching dignity about the little white-clad figure, and there were tears in his eyes. "One day, *espero,* you come back. I wait for that good day when see you again. *Adios. Vayan con Dio, Señores."*

"Well, there's Spanish and Spanish," Simon observed thoughtfully, as they watched the boy march down the sunlit road. "And it takes all kinds to make a world, as the sailor said when he saw a Chinaman. Angelo's a good boy. Hope life treats him right."

Mama Hanno's mouth split in a wide welcoming smile at their approach, and she kept bobbing and gabbling at the same time. Simon listened attentively to the string of words. "She says we've done a good job," he allowed at last. "She is glad Peneranda is dead. He was most wicked man in the world." He listened some more. "She says you have the spirit of both your uncle and Don Diego in you. You have done the right thing to divide what was hidden, to help both peoples. She'll never leave here, but now she can die happy, for Beltran will do well. She wanted us to come so she could say this and thank us for all the people he will care for."

"Thank her for her help to us," mumbled Mark, embarrassed. "Tell her I hope things work out all right."

She said something more and then hobbled over and stood in front of Mark. Putting both hands on his arm she looked earnestly up into his face. "Me no *bruja*," she said very slowly. "But me know you have good fortune *por vida* for brought good fortune to others."

"Why, thank you," Mark said gently. "And good luck to you, too, ma'am." He shook hands and turned down the trail. When Simon joined him they walked back in silence to the stir of the camp.

Tom Davidson met them at the edge of the woods. "Been looking for you." His freckled face was solemn. "I don't figger I rightly know what happened last night, or leastways all of it, or why. Couldn't believe it this morning. But just now I put my hand in my pocket for a piece of rope and I found this." He opened his hand on a glowing ruby.

"Yup," agreed Simon slowly. "I found mine, too." He pulled out a star-shaped pin that winked and glittered like ice.

Tom held his hand toward Mark. "You take it. It's yours."

"No." Mark heard a surprisingly authoritative note in his voice. "That's yours. And Simon's pin's his. You helped me. I wouldn't have that chest, or even be here now, if it hadn't been for you."

Tom's mouth dropped open. "You mean it? Thought you might have been tetched by the moon, or something, when you give it to me. It . . . it might buy me a little farm at that," he added longingly.

"It's yours, of course. But keep it safe."

Tom chuckled, happily. "I'll keep it as safe as the deacon kept the church collection, as Simon would say."

"Weren't going to say that," Simon drawled. "I'm keeping mine as safe as a Mohawk keeps a Huron scalp."

Mark felt his throat tighten. They'd both done so much for him. "There'll be more whenever you want it," he promised. "More, always, for two such friends."

The sun was lying on the rim of the ocean when the transport *Devonshire* dipped her colors to the flag above Morro Castle and set her bow northward. Crowded though she was, Mark and Simon had elbowed their way to her starboard rail. Arms crossed, Mark looked back over the deepening blue of the water to the shore, the British camp with its white tents, the line of green that was the Cavannas, and, farther east, the little point that held Fort Coximar. Beyond that point lay the wide shallows of the bay, and there, beneath a rock, lay half the Peneranda Hoard. And already, ahead of them, speeding north was his share. He hoped he'd done the right thing.

He shut his eyes and saw Uncle Thad's face, weathered, shrewd and kindly. Yes, he'd have done the same thing. He was a fair man. Half for the Peneranda people, half for his own. He'd have been ashamed of himself all his lifetime if he'd taken it all. But he'd have betrayed Uncle Thad and made his death useless if he had not kept half. But he'd have to become much wiser than he was now if the wealth was to do the right kind of good. Perhaps he'd learn at college. Perhaps meeting and listening to wise men would show him what was needed. Perhaps traveling, to see how things were done elsewhere would give him ideas. He'd move slowly, except for Debby. But he had so much to learn.

Simon's shoulder brushed his. "There goes Cuba," Simon drawled. "And I'm as glad to say good-by as the farmer was to say good-by to the skunk. But, at that, Mark," he paused reflectively, "we shouldn't be ungrateful. We come pretty nigh to doing all we aimed to. We got there, and we found the Casas. You won't ever get the places, but that's no more loss to you than a pile of bad potatoes. I saw what I aimed

241

to, the snake that killed Thad get his comeuppance, though I'd kind of figured on doing that myself. Still, it got done. And we found the Peneranda Hoard, and you got your fair share of it. So we didn't do so badly. And look what you got ahead."

Mark spread his hands on the rail, his spirits lifting. Yes . . . ahead. College. Travel. England. France, but he'd learn French first. He'd find what he wanted to do in life. And he could do so much for so many. Why, there wouldn't be time for everything.

"Yup. You got all your life ahead," the homey voice was continuing. "And you've got some memories behind. Some bad. Some good. But most of all you've proved to yourself you're a man and can stand up to anyone and anything. And that's best of all."

Mark gazed ahead to where sky and water melted together. There lay home, and the future, and whatever it might bring. He turned and held out his hand. "But I couldn't have done anything at all without you, Simon. You pushed me here and pulled me there, and helped every time I needed you. I can't thank you enough."

Simon grinned. "I'd a done it for Thad's sake. But, you know, I came to do it for your own. And, you know too, after a time, you weren't looking to me for help; you were looking only to yourself. And that's the way it should be. And now there isn't anyone I'd rather get into trouble with, and out of, than you. We'll have some times ahead. And if this Captain has the spirit of an hour-hooked trout we'll be home in two weeks and can start."

Mark turned back to the dimming shore. Simon was right. They'd done what they set out to do. And he'd learned things about men and about himself he'd never have known if he'd stayed home at Litchfield. The Peneranda Hoard would be helping many people for many years to come. And for him the future was bright and shining. And all because of the silver Peneranda dagger.